DRAGON TALES

This is for Callum

Judy Hayman

This is the third of the Dragon Tales Chronicles.
Already published:
Dragon Tales Book I: Quest for a Cave
Dragon Tales Book II: Quest for a Friend
Coming soon:
Dragon Tales Book IV: The Runaway
Dragon Tales Book V: Dragons in Snow

DRAGON TALES

BOOK III

Quest for Adventure

by

Judy Hayman

illustrated by

Caroline Wolfe Murray

First published in Great Britain by Practical Inspiration
Publishing, 2015

ISBN (print): 978-1-910056-22-6
ISBN (ebook): 978-1-910056-23-3

For my grandsons David and Sam, who also like going
wild on a beach!
J.L.H.

For Benjamin
C.W.M.

Table of Contents

Chapter 1

All About Islands

In the middle of the summer in the Highlands of Scotland it scarcely goes dark all night. On fine evenings the sky is a clear blue, a few stars can be seen, the moon rises huge on the horizon and there is a line of light low in the north and west. Emily and Tom, who had always lived there, were used to this but their friends Alice and Ollie had only just arrived in the Highlands from England and still found it surprising.

The very best thing about summer, as the four young dragons had discovered, was that their parents *sometimes* forgot about bedtime. When it was raining they remembered, and shooed the children off to bed; but on fine evenings like this one, if the four older ones slipped away somewhere they could get away with several extra hours after the little ones, Georgie and Lily, were safely in bed.

This evening they had crept away from Ollie and Alice's home in the wood by the small loch, leaving their four parents talking by the fire. Sometimes Des, their Traveller friend, stayed but often he forgot he was grown up and snuck away with the children. And tonight was special; they had arranged to wake Ben.

They had forgotten everything but the enthralling tales Ben was telling them. As the sky darkened slowly and more stars appeared, Ben's deep voice went on and on. Desmond was sitting quite still on the top of Ben's bald head, listening and gazing into the distance. Tom and Ollie were perched as usual on Ben's ears, though Ollie, who was quite a bit bigger than Tom, was finding it hard to keep his balance. Emily and Alice were sitting comfortably together on Ben's huge hand, which he had raised up in front of his face.

Ben was an ancient Mountain Giant who had spent centuries asleep in this place until he had almost become part of the landscape. In the last few months, with the arrival of Emily's family, who had moved into the cave beneath his chair, and then the English dragons a few weeks later, he had spent more time awake than he had done for many years. It was young company, he explained. There was so much going on! The children had discovered that he didn't really mind if they huffed gently up his nose to wake him up on fine evenings. They had learned not to huff too hard. One giant sneeze could send little dragons whirling through the air in quite a dangerous way!

"Did you know this land was once covered with ice and snow all year round?" Ben was saying. "Even the sea was frozen. Giants could walk for days and see nothing else alive. I tried it for a hundred years or so, but then it seemed like a good time to sleep. So that is what I did. And when I next awoke the ice was gone and the land was green. My legs were younger then, so I walked north over the mountains until I reached the sea. And far over the sea there were islands, hummocky and green. I wanted to reach them, so I started to walk through the sea. Deeper and deeper I went, to my knees, to my waist, and finally to my shoulders. I looked back and I was a long way from the land, but the islands were still far off. What should I do? Even a mountain giant can drown. By this time white waves were tickling my chin!"

"Islands," said Des dreamily from Ben's head. "I love flying to islands..."

"It's easy if you have wings! Unfortunately that's one thing giants don't have," said Ben.

"There wouldn't be any horrible Humans on an island," said Ollie. "They can't fly either. Go on, Ben."

"That's where you're wrong, young Oliver, as I soon found out," Ben continued. "I turned my head this way and that...." He demonstrated, making the boys on his ears wobble and Ollie flap his wings to keep his balance, "...and I saw, coming towards me, six humans bouncing over the waves in a..."

"Boat!" shouted Emily and Alice together. They had read about boats in their books.

"Quite right! They were moving so fast that if I had opened my mouth wide they might have shot in!"

"Yuk!" said Tom, but the others shushed him, wanting Ben to continue.

"Suddenly they realised I was there. I heard screams. The boat lurched and I feared they would fall overboard and drown. But they righted themselves and rowed towards the nearest island as fast as they could. I stood and watched them. The boat looked like a tiny insect with many long legs as it disappeared into the distance. Then I saw wee people gathered on the shore waving and shouting and I realised they could see my head in the sea. I have often wondered what legends they made up about the strange moving rock that appeared one day in the middle of the sea and vanished the next!"

The children chuckled, but Des had a serious question.

"Ben, I've heard of an island that's a home of many dragons far off to the north-west. Do you know about that?"

"I did walk further round the shore and saw more islands to the west, but always the sea was too deep for me to reach them. But once I saw, far far away over the sea, a huge plume of grey smoke and tongues of fire rising high in the sky."

"That's it!" said Desmond excitedly. "There are huge dragons living in caves there, and from time to time they wake up and breathe out fire and smoke. I spoke once with an old Traveller who'd been there. The big dragons were asleep, but he said over all the land you could see little huffs of dragon breath floating through the air. It must be a magical place."

Listening to his voice, Emily realised that the urge to travel was getting stronger and stronger in her friend Desmond. He had stayed with them longer than he had intended, but he was obviously getting itchy wings as he listened to Ben. She hated the thought of waving goodbye to him. He was such great company, with his coloured spikes and his fancy cooking, his love of exploring and the wild tales of his adventures.

"Hmm," came Ben's voice, "I have never been there, of course, but I believe the place is called Ice Land and is far out in the Western Sea. Chilly by the sound of it, and so NOT a suitable place for dragons." He rolled his eyes to look up at Des and gave a deep rumbling chuckle. "Tell me all about it when you get back," he said, and closed his eyes.

"Des, you can't go!" said all the young dragons together.

"I must, I'm a Traveller — and I've stayed here far too long! I really like the sound of this Ice Land place." He yawned widely. "Needs a bit of planning though. Tomorrow. Come on, you'd better go down before they start looking for you."

They said goodnight to Ben — who waved his hand with his eyes shut once Emily and Alice had flown up — and made their way home: Alice and Ollie to their woodland camp and Emily and Tom to their cave.

"See you tomorrow," said Alice as they left. Des waved to them, then disappeared inside the grubby bag he slept in and said no more about plans or islands.

It had been a lovely evening, Emily thought as she snuggled down in her heather bed. But the thought of losing Desmond had spoiled it. It was a long time before she fell asleep, and when she did she dreamed of islands that smoked and the wide wild sea.

Chapter 2

Desmond's Parting Gift

Emily was woken early by the sound of clanking. She guessed what it was and crawled out of bed to check. Sure enough, Des was collecting his strange assortment of cooking gear into bundles. He was leaving.

"Oh Des — you're not going *today!*"

"Tonight. I prefer night flying. There are a few things I want to do before I leave."

"Will we ever see you again?" Emily felt like bursting into tears. Des put a wing round her and gave her a hug.

"Course you will! You'll still be living in this cave, right? So I'll come back after I've been to Ice Land and tell you all about it. When you're a bit older you can come travelling too. Tell you what — if I find a good place by the sea that's not too far away, I'll take you there. You and the others. How's that? Cheer up. I've a surprise for you and Alice before I go."

Emily sniffed back her tears and busied herself lighting the fire before her parents and Tom woke up. Des started rolling up his grubby sleeping bag and she was helping him to tie it up when her parents and baby Lily emerged from their sleeping cave. Tom was still fast asleep after his late night, and Emily was just in time to catch Lily before she went back in to jump on him.

Over breakfast, Des explained his plans to Mum and Dad, and then he flew down to the camp to tell Ellen and Oliver. Emily realised that, although the others were staying in their woodland camp for the rest of the summer, there had been no discussion of what they would do when winter came. Desmond could always find her in Ben's cave, but it would be more difficult for him to find Alice and Ollie. She felt more and more depressed. After this lovely summer with so many friends, it would be horrible to lose them.

After they had helped with the washing up, she and Tom flew to the camp. They heard the argument that was taking place even before they landed.

"I AM old enough to go with Des!" Ollie was shouting. "It's not fair! I bet you were travelling when you were my age, weren't you?" he said to Des, who was shaking his head.

"Not where I'm going," said Des. "Too dangerous. Sorry Ollie. But I've promised Emily I'll look out for a place near the sea to take you all when I get back. I know she wants to see the sea."

"We've seen the sea lots of times," said Ollie sulkily.

"Not wild *Scottish* sea. It's quite different from anything you'll have seen."

"I bet you forget. You'll get to Ice Land and then go on somewhere else and never come back." Ollie was so furious that he sent a jet of flame into the dry grass near the camp and then stomped off, leaving his parents to stamp out the fire. Ellen sighed.

"Leave him to calm down," she said. "But I do hope you'll come back while we're still here, Des. Right you three, make the most of Desmond's last day. Take him swimming."

They enjoyed a good long swim in the big loch with the young otters, who were now almost as big as their parents and could only fly over the loch on Desmond's back one at a time. They were sleek and fast, and won every swimming race, even when they gave the dragons a good start. Eventually they said they had to go fishing, and left the exhausted dragons panting and dripping on the bank.

When they had dried off, Des led them to a clearing in the woods and went to fetch a bundle from his pack. When he came back he showed them some coloured dyes.

"Who wants some coloured spikes like mine?" he said cheerfully. "Mine have faded a bit, but they're still pretty cool. I used every one of these colours, but you can choose whatever you like!"

Emily and Alice looked at one another, tempted.

"Yes please!" said Alice.

"All right," said Emily, who had secretly liked the idea when Des had first arrived, though she was not sure her mother would approve.

"Yuck, no way!" said Tom. "If you're going to mess around with that, I'm going to find Ollie."

Emily and Des looked thoughtfully at Alice. She was an English dragon, pinkish red with wings shaded orange. "If I have blue spikes I might look a little bit Scottish like Emily," she decided. Des carefully painted her spikes in different shades of blue, though he said that rainbow colours like his would have been better.

"Rainbow for you Emily?" he asked hopefully when Alice was finished and admiring her reflection in the still waters of the loch.

"No," she said. "I'd like some spikes pink to go with the shading on my wings, and some green."

"Green like me?"

"Sludgy green you mean?" said Alice, pulling a face.

"Cheek!"

"A nice green, like my Gran. That one's pretty," Emily decided, ignoring them.

Des shook his head in despair as he opened the pot she'd chosen.

"Sure I can't give you both orange tails?" he said when Emily was finished and pleased with her new look.

"No thanks!" they said together.

"We like to be tasteful," Alice explained.

At that moment, Tom and Ollie reappeared. Tom stared at the girls and then rolled about on the grass, laughing. But he stopped and looked as if he might change his mind when Ollie said, "Yeah, Des — you can paint me BLACK — spikes *and* tail. That'll show them!"

Alice sighed, but Des happily opened his pot of black and set to work on Ollie's spikes.

There was surprisingly little fuss about the new spikes when they went back to the camp later in the day. They had flown down the valley for Des to take a last look at the ancient castle ruins that crowned a hillock within it — and to give the new colours time to set, in case the parents tried to make them wash the paint off. They scouted carefully for wandering Humans before flying down to the ruins, but as usual the glen was empty and peaceful. They had all heard Ben's tale of the great battle by this time.

"It's a good thing there's hardly anything left of this old place," said Desmond thoughtfully. "If a few walls were left standing this glen would be overrun by Humans. The stones are disappearing under the moss and heather."

When they strolled casually into the camp late in the afternoon there were exclamations of surprise but no real annoyance. Emily decided that Ollie was disappointed. He had strutted into camp ahead of the others, looking, she thought, rather dramatic, the black dye a striking contrast to his red scales. Des had carefully edged his wings as well as blackening his spikes. Oliver opened his mouth and huffed ominously until a sharp nudge from his wife's tail made him shut it again. The mothers actually admired their daughters' new spikes.

"I could do yours too," Des offered, but they declined, laughing.

"Leave it to the youngsters," Gwen said. "And Tom, I'm quite glad you're still plain blue!"

"I've one more thing to suggest before I leave," Des said, leading them into the wood. He stopped beside an old oak tree with a gnarled trunk and thick branches that spread widely all round. It had grown wide rather than tall, as oaks often do in the Highlands.

"This is a fantastic place for a tree house!" he said. "You've got lots of time to build it while I'm away. I'll check it out when I get back, before we go to the sea. So that's a promise. I'll be back!"

They had a splendid farewell feast: crow and toad-stool stew with crispy fried slugs, and thistles dipped in honey and nettle knights to finish with. Desmond gave Gwen and Ellen a few of his spicy pods and seeds to hot up their cooking, and they presented him with a bag of his favourite bumblebugs.

"When you finish them you'll *have* to come back for more!" Emily said.

"That'll be next week if you eat them two at a time as you usually do!" said Tom, making them all laugh.

Carrying Georgie and Lily, they all flew up to Ben's head to see Desmond off as the sun slowly set behind the mountains.

"YEAY! Ice Land here I come!" he shouted as he took off, and he huffed a huge smoke ring high into the air. They all waved and cheered as the oddly shaped dragon, hung with bundles as Emily had first seen him, disappeared into the gloaming, huffing smoke rings as he went.

"Bye bye!" shouted little Georgie, and Lily squeaked and jumped on her father's back, waving her wings and making them all laugh. Emily looked round at her family and all her friends and felt better.

"Let's start the tree house in the morning," she said, and everyone agreed as they made their way down to the cave and the camp.

Chapter 3

The Tree House

Unfortunately it was raining the following day. The heavy grey clouds were so low that they seemed to sit on the top of Ben's bald head. When Emily peered out in the morning, she recognised the sort of Highland day where the rain would never stop.

"Dreich day!" said Dad, coming in with dripping wings.

It was too wet to light the fire outside, so they had a cold breakfast inside the cave. Tom argued with his parents and then sulked because they said it was too wet to start the building of the tree house. "It might rain for weeks!" he argued. "We don't mind the wet. We're dragons! We won't melt!"

Emily was trying to decide whether to agree with him for a change — he was right about the wet and she secretly thought her parents were being too fussy — when there was a flurry outside the cave and Alice and Ollie landed and shook the worst of the rain off their wings and tails.

"Can we come in?" said Alice. "It's far too wet to start building, but we thought we could do some planning in here where it's dry."

Tom and Emily cheered up immediately and, to their parents' relief, they all crammed into Emily's private bedroom cave. "If they don't start fighting in there, we should have peace for a morning," said Gwen.

In Emily's room there was a smooth piece of cave wall that Ollie said was perfect for drawing. Alice produced a few white pebbles, and they spent a happy morning designing tree houses, which grew more and more complicated and fantastic as time went on. Finally the girls said Tom's latest effort was *much* too stupid, and the boys retreated to Tom's cave to make plans of their own, which they said were private. The girls let them go with relief. They stared thoughtfully at the drawings on the wall.

"That one?" said Alice.

Emily nodded. "Whichever we choose, we'll need the grown-ups to help, whatever Ollie says. Even he can't carry heavy pieces of wood."

"We'd better start being nice to the parents then," said Alice, and went to warn Ollie and Tom to be on their best behaviour for a change. Outside the clouds were beginning to lift.

The grown-ups seemed happy to help in the building of the tree house in the oak that Desmond had chosen. Even Ollie agreed that they were needed to carry big straight logs to make a floor, and sometimes they used their spiked tails to chop them to the right size. Then the youngsters wove smaller branches together to make walls and even managed to make two small windows, though the boys secretly thought that was a bit too fussy. Finally a good roof was constructed in the higher branches and tied on with long strands of tough old ivy. A nice flat branch at the front made an excellent landing place when its sprouting twigs had been cut away.

All this took many days, and by the end, the parents left them to it. The boys decided it was finished long before Emily and Alice were satisfied, so eventually they went off fishing for the day leaving the girls to themselves. "Fussing around decorating! Typical!" they said as they set off for the otters' loch.

Emily and Alice gazed happily round the big square room they had constructed and tidied stray bits of twig into the walls. Alice looked critically at the opening they had left for the entrance.

"Can we hang something up there?" she suggested. "It would make it more of a secret hide-out."

"Big bracken fronds might work," said Emily, and they set off to collect some. When they had carefully fastened them in the entrance the fronds formed a thick green curtain, so that the inside of their tree-house became dim and mysterious.

"Something soft to sit on next," said Alice. "Heather. Then we need some decorations. How about strings of fir cones? "

"Thistle flowers would look nice. Or gorse...?" They went off into the woods, thinking hard.

They had threaded some thistle heads and flowering gorse into the walls and were arranging two neat piles of heather beside the far wall when they heard voices outside. "I think we'd better knock," said Gwen. "It looks as though they want to keep their house private!"

Alice and Emily peered out. "Come and see what we've done," said Emily and their mothers squeezed through the bracken curtain to admire the inside. It was a bit of a squash with four of them inside, and seemed even smaller when Lily and Georgie, who had followed them up, scampered in and started to scatter the neat heather seats as they bounced around in excitement.

"Can we sleep in here tonight? Please!" asked Alice.

"I don't see why not," said her mother. "It's not too far from the camp if you need anything in the night. What about the boys?"

Emily and Alice looked at each other. "I suppose so," they agreed. "But they can collect their own heather beds. And if they can't be bothered, they can just sleep on the floor!"

Gwen laughed and pointed to the heather pile. "I think you have two squatters as well!" she said. Lily and Georgie had burrowed inside and were pretending to be asleep. "We'll just leave them, shall we?"

Alice and Emily looked doubtful and Ellen laughed. "Don't worry, we won't make you babysit. They're far too young to sleep up a tree. You can let them in to play sometimes, for a treat, if they promise to behave. Are you listening, Georgie?" There was a cheeky huff from under the heather.

At that moment, two thumps on the landing branch announced the arrival of the boys, who pulled several bracken strands loose as they barged in. Ollie scowled.

"What are they doing here? I thought we'd agreed no parents allowed. And certainly no kids," he added, catching sight of a wriggling heap of heather at the back of the room.

"Calm down, Ollie! We're not planning to stay. Did you catch any fish?"

"Lots," said Tom proudly.

"Are you planning to cook them yourselves? You seem to have banned parents from interfering..."

"Erm..." said Ollie.

"Course not!" said Tom, surprised. "We can have them for supper, can't we? I think there's enough. That OK, Ollie?"

"Suppose so."

Gwen and Ellen smiled at the girls and Tom, pointedly ignored Ollie and squeezed their way out, taking a sleepy Lily with them. Georgie scampered after them and slid down the tree trunk to the ground.

"We're going to sleep in here tonight," said Emily.

"Us too?" asked Tom eagerly.

"Pretty good beds," Ollie admitted, sitting down on the nearest one.

"Yes. Ours." said Alice. "But there's plenty of heather up the hillside. Mind the door as you go out this time."

The boys sighed heavily, then pushed with exaggerated care through the bracken doorway and flew away. Alice and Emily grinned at each other.

"High Four?" said Alice. They clapped wings.

Chapter 4

Desmond at Sea

Four days after leaving Ben McIlwhinnie and his friends in Scotland, Des was wishing he was back. He sat shivering on a tiny rocky island in the middle of a heaving grey sea, sucking a bumblebug and wondering what to do next. All around him, big seabirds were wheeling and shrieking without a care in the world. It was all right for them, he thought. When they got tired they could have a rest, floating on the sea. But he had to keep going until he felt as though his wings would fall off. He had never been so miserable.

The fact was that Des had never flown so far over water before. Although he had travelled a long way south, he had never had to cross miles and miles of sea. The travellers' tales that he had enjoyed telling Emily and the others over the summer had been — well — a bit exaggerated perhaps. A bit less dangerous than they had sounded! But he hated the thought of going back and confessing that he had never reached Ice Land at all.

If only there were a few sticks on this wretched rock, he could get a fire going and warm up. He had huffed some smoke and a bit of flame just to warn the seabirds off, but that didn't help to keep him warm, and he had a feeling that they wouldn't keep away for long. He knew they ate fish, but wasn't convinced they might not try Dragon for a change.

He was counting his remaining bumblebugs and working out how to make them last when he spotted one of the largest of the birds — dark brown with a hooked beak and a fierce eye — sidling closer over the rock. It ducked its head a few times in greeting and spoke in a harsh voice.

"Whit ur you? No' seen a burd like you afore!"

"I'm not a bird. I'm a dragon. What're you?"

"Bonxie. We're the heid burds roond here. Naebdy messes wi' us. Where ye headin'?"

"Ice Land. Have you been there? Is it much further? I've flown from Scotland. Not too sure of the way."

"Aye, Ah ken the place. Lang way, and nae mair wee islands on the way frae now on."

"I can't float on the sea for a rest like you can. That's the problem."

"Get a ride on yin o' they floatin' hooses. Tha's whit lots o' th' wee burdies dae. The human folk gie them food. Nae danger."

"I can't. Humans don't believe in dragons. They'd put me in a cage and ship me to a zoo!"

"Right... bit o' a problem there, pal! Tell ye whit. I'm away tae Ice Land masel'. Fur the fishin', ye ken. Ah c'n tak ye the quickest way."

Desmond could hardly believe his luck. Hoping he wasn't making the biggest mistake of his life, he checked his baggage — to the bewilderment of the Bonxie, which simply spread its wings — and prepared to fly.

It was a very long way! Fortunately the Bonxie knew all about the local airways, and was able to take him high enough to rest his wings by riding the current. There was no sign of land ahead when the Bonxie decided they should float for a while, persuading Des that as long as kept his wings high and dry he would manage. Des wasn't at all sure, but had no choice but to follow his guide in a long glide down to the surface of the sea, which still looked unpleasantly grey.

They were very close to the surface when, to Des's horror, a huge creature heaved itself out of the sea and blew a fountain of water at him. It was black and shiny and flicked a massive tail as it disappeared below the waves. He almost fell into the sea with fright. Then he realised that the Bonxie was yelping with laughter.

"Ha' ye no' seen yin o' them whales afore? Nae need to be feart o' them. They cannae fly. Right noo. Can ye land wi'oot getting yer wings a' drookit?" It landed neatly on the water and folded its wings.

Des hovered uncertainly for a few seconds, then landed beside the Bonxie and paddled his legs furiously. To his surprise, if he kept his head and wings high and clear of the waves, he could paddle more gently and still keep afloat. His legs needed some exercise, he decided — it was his wings that deserved a rest! He didn't dare go to sleep as the Bonxie did, tucking its head beneath its wing, but when it was time to fly on, he felt fit enough to go.

Very early one morning, the mountainous shape of Ice Land loomed ahead of them. Des thought he saw a high smoke signal rising up from a mountain in the distance, but he was really too exhausted to care as long as he could find a place to sleep — preferably for a week. They flew lower as the land came nearer, and Des could see that a good deal of the middle of the huge island seemed to be black or white, but it was green round the edge. Waves were breaking on stony beaches, and hundreds of seabirds flew around and above them as they finally came in to land.

Des flopped in an untidy heap on the shingle, too exhausted even to look around him. Fortunately the Bonxie was wide awake. Dimly Des heard it laying down the law to the assembled flocks.

"Right, ah ken this beastie's a daft shape, and naw, he isnae a parrot for a' his fancy colours. He says he's a DRAGON, name o' Des. Onyways, he's a pal o' mine and there'll be nae divebombin', nae peckin', nae pooin', nae nickin' his grub, and ye'll a' leave him alane 'til he's rested, right? RIGHT?"

There was a confused babble from the collected birds, but opening one eye, Des could see that they had backed away from him and the Bonxie, which was standing on a rock beside him making stabbing motions with its powerful beak. Some took to the air and headed out to sea.

"Thanks," he murmured.

"Nae bother. But Ah wouldnae stay here if ye need to keep oot o' sight o' humans. When the sun's up there'll likely be some paddlin' alang here."

Des groaned. "I usually hide up a tree," he said.

"Nae trees roond here. Thirz a wee cave along a bit, mind. Would that dae ye fur a bit o' kip?"

Des heaved himself to his feet, his wings drooping. "If you don't mind, I'll walk," he said, and followed the Bonxie as it flew ahead in short bursts from rock to rock. The cave entrance proved to be low and narrow, with only just enough room for him to squeeze himself in, but it was higher inside and there was a small patch of flat sandy floor. "Perfect!" he said gratefully, flopping down again.

"See y' aroond," the Bonxie said preparing for take-off, but Des was already fast asleep.

Chapter 5

Disappointment for Des

Desmond had no idea how long he slept, but when he woke up, hungry and thirsty, the cave was pitch black. He got to his feet, stretched and tried to remember the way out. He sent up a tiny huff of flame to give himself some light and crawled towards the entrance. To his horror, it was blocked by a large dark boulder.

Des tiptoed cautiously up to the stone hoping he could climb over it. There was certainly not enough space to crawl round the side. He stretched out a claw and had another shock; the boulder was warm and soft! It didn't take him long to work out that a large seal had gone to sleep at the cave entrance and shut him in. Unfortunately, as he knew from his travels, seals could sleep for hours and were very hard to shift. He was too thirsty to wait for it to wake up.

Kicks and prods had no effect, and it wasn't until he backed into the cave, spread his wings and took a flying leap onto its back that the seal gave a grunt and rolled over, nearly knocking him off in the process. It was late afternoon and the beach was full of seals. His was the biggest and it barked menacingly and showed its teeth, so he decided to fly away from the colony in search of a drink, leaving his belongings in the cave for the present. He snatched a clawful of seaweed for emergency rations as he took off.

It wasn't hard to find a stream and after a long drink, followed by a snack of seaweed, which he dried and crisped with huff, he felt better.

There must be more to Ice Land than seals and birds, he decided. Time to look for the famous Dragons and that smoke signal he'd spotted on the flight in!

The cliff behind the beach was quite low, and when he peered over the top he saw a wide expanse of green dotted with black rocks, and, to his horror, some scattered Human houses. Obviously he would have to travel very carefully.

He kept a sharp look-out as he scrambled between the rocks and allowed himself short bursts of low flying, heading inland. In the distance he could see what looked like an inland cliff with a strange white edge, and a number of waterfalls looking like white threads tumbling to the plain. There was one wide fall a little nearer. Des loved waterfalls! He decided to risk a longer flight.

It was nearly a disaster.

Not far inland was a road, screened by low bushes, which he didn't see until he was nearly on top of it. During his travels Des had learned that the Human things that ran along roads were not really dangerous, as the Humans inside sped past too fast to catch sight of him. But this time, a much larger vehicle was standing at the side of the road, and a number of Humans, wearing bright clothes and woolly hats, were standing around, gazing through binoculars or pointing cameras at a little herd of small hairy horses, all different colours, which seemed to be posing for them. Des swerved and tried to speed away, but he was too late. There was a shout from the group. He risked a look back, and saw that now they were all pointing and gazing at HIM! He hoped very much that nobody had a gun.

As fast as he could he headed for a tumble of rocks in the distance, and disappeared behind them, shaking with fear. Peering through a gap he saw the Humans, some still looking in his direction, climb back into their bus, which roared away.

He huddled under an overhanging rock, still shaking, and decided to stay there until dark. He finished his seaweed and wished he had remembered to bring some bumblebugs with him, to take away the strong salty taste. There didn't seem to be any snails around either.

Darkness was a long time coming. In fact it hardly came at all. The sun left a glow in the sky to the west as Des crawled out of his hiding place and cautiously set off towards the nearest waterfall. It was huge — far bigger than any he had seen before. He longed to fly through it, as he had done so often, but he was shaken after his narrow escape from the Humans and the seal and for once decided not to risk being dashed down to the boiling pool at the bottom of the cliff. There was nobody around to impress, after all!

Instead he flew to the top and landed beside the fall. Instead of the river he had expected, water was pouring from underneath the white ground. When he tried to walk on the surface, he slithered and near-ly tumbled into a deep crack that seemed to shine with a weird greenish light. After a short flight low over the uneven grey and white landscape, he decided there was no chance any self-respecting dragon would live in this cold wilderness. The famous fire-breathers must live somewhere else.

For quite a while he flew on, skirting the edge of the huge glacier until he came to a wide green valley that seemed to be empty of Humans. He was very excited when he realised that all over the hillside opposite, tiny puffs of white smoke were rising in the air. This must be it! Under this land there was a nest of dragons, all huffing away. All he had to do was find the entrance to their cave....

He searched until the sun came up, but there was no sign of a cave. He went from one to another of the huffs, but they just seemed to come out of the earth. Sometimes a bigger plume of smoke would erupt, and he would fly over as fast as he could, but nowhere was there any sight or sound of another dragon.

When he heard the ominous rumble of Human traffic from a hidden road he decided it was time to lie low for the day.

He headed back towards the sea, flew along the shore as fast as he could and finally saw the opening of his cave. There was no seal in the way, though there were still plenty of them on the beach. He crouched in the entrance and blew a defiant fiery huff to deter invaders before scrambling inside, checking his bundles and falling thankfully asleep.

(His huff was spotted by a two fishermen in a small boat in the bay. They steered a little closer to shore to see if it happened again, then decided they must have been seeing things...)

When Des woke up it was evening and the Bonxie was preening its feathers at the entrance to the cave.

"Thought ye'd niver wake up!" it said, dropping two small eels beside him. "Huv ye foond ony mair dragons?"

As he chewed the eels, Des told him of his disappointing search, and confessed that he had been spotted by some Humans.

"Aye, ah kin see thirz bin folk around the day. Selkies've gone an' thiz prints in the sand, ken. Could've bin lookin' fur you. Good thing this cave's too wee fur 'em. Onyways, bin askin' aroond fur ye, an' a pal o' mine sez there might be a dragon bidin' up the big mountain o'er yonder. Want me ter tak ye up there fur a wee keek?"

Des scrambled out of the cave in a hurry and followed the Bonxie as it took off. This time he remembered to take his bumblebugs!

They flew high and fast towards the middle of the island heading for the higher ground. The high smoke signal came nearer, but it seemed to be getting fainter, and wavering in the wind as they headed towards it. The Bonxie came to land on a high rock before they reached it, and Des landed alongside.

"Is that yer dragon breathin'?" it said.

Des looked doubtfully at the smoke, which was still quite a way off.

"If it is, it must be the biggest dragon in the world!" he said. "Have you never heard of a huge flying dragon round here? It must come out sometimes."

"Naa, niver. An' ahd've heard if one'd flown o'er here. Thirz no' much Ah dinnae ken aboot this place. Tell ye whit. Ah think it's no' a dragon, it's the Land. Ah've seen white smoke, 'n' black smoke sae thick you couldnae fly though it, 'n' hot orange rivers crawlin' o'er the land. If it wasnae fur the fishin' Ah'd no' bother comin' at a'. Even thae humans seem feart o' this place."

Des gazed at the plume of smoke, and remembered the wispy huffs in the valley. "Perhaps you're right," he admitted rather sadly. "I hoped I'd discover a whole host of dragons here. It's rather lonely being a dragon, and because we're so rare we're always in danger from humans. You wouldn't understand. There are hundreds of Bonxies around, so you're not in any danger."

"Aye, that's true, but Ah ken ither kinds o' burds that're rare like you. They huv tae look oot fur their eggs 'n' chicks. I've heard some humans watch oot fur them, but Ah wouldnae ken aboot that. If Ah see humans near ma nest Ah'll go fur 'em, nae danger. Want tae heid back?"

"Can we go up and check first?"

They flew up towards the smoke, and circled the top of the mountain warily. There was a horrible smell, and they could see that the smoke was coming from a large crater near the top of the mountain. The land around was black and barren, with rocks twisted into fantastic shapes. The sight and the smell finally convinced Des that no dragon could live in this bleak place, and he agreed that it was time to go.

The sun was rising as they headed back to the coast and as they neared their beach they realised that something was wrong. Every seabird in the area was wheeling and screeching above the beach, and out to sea they could see the heads of seals that should have been stretched out and basking in the sun. As they flew over the cliff edge they saw why. A group of Humans had invaded their beach!

Des backpedalled furiously and landed behind a rock.

"What can I do?" he moaned. "All my stuff is in the cave!"

"Ach, ye dinnae need stuff!" the Bonxie said. "Ah'll fly oot and see whit they're up tae."

It was back in a few minutes.

"Nae guid. Yin's lyin' doon an' shinin' a thingy intae the cave. They cannae get in, o' course, but Ah reckon they ken ye've bin there."

There was a sudden loud barking and the Bonxie flew up again.

"Och, the've brought a dug! That'll get in fur sure. Time to get goin', pal!"

"I can't go without my stuff!"

The Bonxie rolled its eyes. "Nae wonder dragons've near deid oot! All ye need is yur wings, pal. Dinnae fash, I'll call the lads."

Ten minutes later, a small flock of Great Skuas gathered and on a count of three, followed their leader down to the beach. Peering cautiously over the cliff edge, Des saw them dive onto the Humans, snapping their beaks and screaming menacingly, then soar out of reach before diving again. It wasn't long before all the Humans, and their terrified dog, were hurrying away from the cave, pursued by the Skuas. Several of them were decorated with white streaks, he noticed, chuckling.

The Bonxie came back as its friends followed the departing Humans, screaming in triumph.

"Right, get goin' while ye can, pal. Scotland's a better place fur dragons." They scrambled down to the cave, where Des collected his belongings and thanked the Bonxie for all its help.

"Pleasure, pal. See ye aroond!" The Bonxie flew high and signalled that it was safe for Des to fly away. Heaving a sigh of relief, Des took off and headed out to sea.

"DRAGON OR HOAX?" proclaimed the Icelandic newspaper headlines next day, under a blurry photograph of a tiny dragon-shaped object in the sky. But fortunately Des knew nothing of this as he thankfully headed for home.

Chapter 6

A Mysterious Message

On the first sleepover in their new tree house, the four young dragons stayed awake late into the night, telling creepy stories about ghostly dragons and sinister Humans. In the morning, the sun shining through the chinks in the walls woke them very early. So it was not surprising that they were inclined to be grumpy at breakfast time. It was Old George who suggested an expedition up the hill in the afternoon.

"You can look for berries and beetles on the way up," he said. "And if you stay 'til the gloaming, you could send up a Huff. You never know, Desmond may be on his way back. He's been gone quite a while, and I'm sure he won't want to spend too long in Ice Land. It sounds far too chilly even for a doughty Traveller like Des."

"I have a horrible feeling something's happened to him," said Emily. "What if he's been caught? Or fallen into the sea?"

"Naa, not Des! But he's probably found lots of exciting new friends there," said Tom gloomily.

"If he has he won't want to come back here," Ollie agreed.

"You never know," said Alice. "He did promise. Anyway, let's go up and try. Can we take a picnic, Mum?"

Carrying a bag of slugs and snails to roast on a fire at the top, and another to fill with berries, they set off, soaring over the heather and gorse in the sunshine. A pair of hunting buzzards circled over them, and the four little dragons took it in turns to fly up and huff smoke and flame to scare them off. It didn't work. The birds just flew higher in lazy circles, giving their mewing cries to each other as they flew.

"Ignore them. They'll go away," said Ollie, after his final attempt had failed. They flew closer together and nearer to the ground. Suddenly, with a shriek, the female bird dived down, talons outstretched, scattering the dragons. In panic they landed in a heap in the bracken and she flew back to join her mate. Now the mewing cries sounded suspiciously like sniggers.

The four dragons picked themselves up, disentangled their tails and collected up their scattered food. Somehow even Ollie didn't feel like flying on just yet, so they crawled through the high bracken searching for beetles and trying to pretend that they had planned this all along. It was Alice who spotted the crows: four of them, flying straight at the buzzards, weaving and harrying them so that they were forced off course. When several more flew to join in, the buzzards gave up and soared away over the hill. The four dragons stood on an outcrop of rock and cheered loudly, until Emily suggested that the crows might turn on them next. Hurriedly they jumped off the rock and resumed their beetle hunt.

The crows soon flew away, leaving the sky clear, so they flew on keeping low to the ground, until they came to a stream bubbling between peaty banks. After a refreshing drink, and a quick check to see that there was nothing lurking in the sky, they flew to the top of the hill. Here the ground was stony and it was safe to collect old bracken stalks and build a small fire. They all gathered round to huff it alight, and speared their food on stalks to roast.

When they had finished it was still a bit early for smoke signals, but they found a good patch of blaeberries (Alice and Ollie called them whinberries, and said they grew in England too) and foraged happily until they had all eaten a good many and their bag was nearly full.

The sun was low in the sky when they gathered on the highest rock on the hilltop and prepared for the biggest Huff they could manage between them. It wasn't bad, as a joint effort, though it was not nearly as high a column of smoke as Emily and her parents had managed on the night they had contacted Desmond for the first time. When they ran out of breath they gazed eagerly towards the north, hoping for a cheerful Huff from Des to say he was on his way back. But there was nothing, and their column of smoke broke up and drifted away in the wind.

They looked at each other, disappointed. "Try again?" said Alice, and they huffed even harder, but still there was no answering column of smoke in the distance.

"Let's try once more and, this time, look in all directions," suggested Ollie. "After all, he might have come the long way round." Nobody else had thought of this, and their hopes revived.

As the last column drifted upwards, they stood back to back and peered in four quarters of the sky. To their surprise it was Tom, who was facing south, who pointed and gave a shout. "Look, look, there he is!"

They all swung round to stare. Instead of a thin column of white smoke like theirs, they saw, far away, a series of small puffs with gaps in between.

"What's he saying? D'you think he needs help?" asked Tom, bewildered.

Then Emily produced her big surprise.

"It says - *we're coming as fast as we can should arrive tomorrow*," she said. The others looked at her in astonishment.

"I didn't know you could read Huff!" said Alice.

"Mum's been teaching me," said Emily, proudly.

"Never mind that," said Ollie impatiently. "Is it Des? Why does he say *we?* Can you send a reply? Ask who it is."

Feeling even more pleased with herself, Emily flew to the top of a high rock, perched precariously, and sent her smoke signal into the dusk. A few minutes later the answer came back. She read it and jumped down, looking puzzled.

"Well?" said the other three. Tom hopped impatiently.

"I'm pretty sure it isn't Des. It said - *its a surprise wait and see shouldnt you be in bed*."

"That doesn't sound like Des at all. Who on earth can it be?" asked Alice.

Ollie took charge. "No idea, but it sounds as though we'll find out. I only hope we like whoever it is. Not someone who fusses about bedtime! Still, I suppose we'd better get back before it gets any darker. We don't want search parties out."

They all agreed, collected their bags and set off down the hill. This time they were not bothered by birds, though Ollie kept an eye out for owls just in case. They had no breath left for talking as they glided fast and straight down to the camp, where they found Duncan waiting to take Emily and Tom back to their cave for the night.

Before they left, Alice whispered, "Will you teach me Huff, Emily?" but Ollie signalled urgently that they should keep the huffed message a secret.

Nodding to show they agreed, Emily and Tom flew off with their Dad, leaving the others to ponder the mystery until the morning.

Chapter 7

Visitors

It was quite hard to keep the secret when they got home. Emily nearly gave the game away when she burst in to tell her mother how useful it was that she had learned to read Huff, but a sharp prod from Tom's tail, which made her jump, stopped her. She was worried that her parents would ask awkward questions, but to her relief they said nothing about huffed messages and just produced hot mint tea before shooing Tom and Emily to bed.

When they got up next morning they were surprised to find that their parents had been awake and busy for some time. The cave seemed unusually tidy. They were bursting to discuss the mysterious message with Alice and Ollie, so they bolted their breakfast and prepared to fly to the camp.

Irritatingly, their parents found a number of jobs for them to do before they left. There was water to fetch, nettles to pick and pine branches to jump into the right size of sticks for the fire. Usually Tom enjoyed jumping sticks, but today he was in a hurry to be off. Just as he finished his heap, and Emily had swept it into a neater pile with her tail so they could leave, their mother came out to say that Tom's room needed tidying and Lily wanted Emily to tell her a story.

Sighing heavily, Tom protested that he liked his room the way it was, but his mother said the guddle was even worse than usual, and shoved him inside. Lily pulled Emily into her room and snuggled down happily, giving small huffs of excitement, so that Emily hadn't the heart to say no. Listening to bangs and thumps from Tom's room, she set out to make her story exciting but short, and when she heard him rush out again, she hurried the ending and followed him.

"Can we go NOW?" she heard him demand as she scrambled out, followed by Lily who was squeaking "Mo, mo!" as she went. To her surprise, her mother was staring intently into the sky and her father was nowhere to be seen. A long thin plume of smoke was rising, and she realised that he was Huffing from the top of Ben's head.

"What's going on?" she and Tom shouted together.

Their mother made no reply, but carried on gazing upwards. Then Emily's sharp eyes spotted two tiny dots in the sky. As she watched, they got bigger until she realised they were two dragons, flying slowly towards them. Her mother waved her wings excitedly, then took off and flew to meet them. Suddenly Emily guessed who they were.

"It's the Gramps!" she breathed in astonishment.

"It's not Des!" Tom said at the same time. Then, "Who?"

"Nan and Edward! Our Gramps, from Wales! That's brilliant!" Emily jumped up and down in excitement.

"I'd rather it was Des," Tom sounded disappointed and Emily remembered that he had never met his grandparents.

"You'll love them, Tom," she said, and soared up into the air to meet them.

There was such a bustle of wings and tails and huffs of smoke when all five dragons landed outside the cave that Lily was frightened and ran inside to hide. Tom also backed away, as Emily flung her wings round first one of the elderly dragons, then the other and hugged them happily.

"Mum, you never said they were coming!" she cried. "Did you know?"

"We had a Huff yesterday, while you were out," said her mother. "But we decided to keep it as a surprise. We didn't know they were planning it." She went into the cave to find Lily, while Duncan brought water for the travellers, who were recovering their breath and gazing around.

"And you must be Tom. What a lovely bright blue you are!" said Nan, giving him a hug. Tom was feeling shy and was unnaturally quiet, thought Emily.

"I think someone else spotted our signals yesterday," said Edward. "Could it have been one of you?" His eyes twinkled at Tom and Emily. "Someone has been learning Huff."

"I spotted it!" shouted Tom, recovering. "But only Emily could read it."

"I thought it would be you," said Nan, giving Emily another hug. "Clever girl!"

"And this is our little Lily," said Mum, carrying her out of the cave. "Say hello to your Gramps, Lily."

Lily sat up and gave them each a little huff, then hid under her mother's wing. Everybody laughed.

"It won't last," said Duncan. She's never shy for more than five minutes, is she, Emily?"

"No," said Emily. "She's much too bossy."

"She's beautiful," said Nan. "I don't think we've ever had a golden dragon in the family have we, Edward?"

"She matches my spikes!" said Edward proudly, and Nan chuckled. She was green, but Edward was blue with touches of Irish gold on spikes and wings.

"I can't remember having a child with coloured spikes either," Nan added. "Very pretty, Emily! I have a feeling a friend of ours has been visiting you."

"Of course, you know Des!" said Emily. "I remember him saying you were the sparkiest dragon he

knew, Gran. He stayed for ages, but he's gone away now. We want him to come back."

"He will. In fact, he's on his way. He sent us a message on the Gloaming Huff and suggested we paid you a visit in your new cave," said Edward. "So we decided to come before we get too old to fly so far. It's taken us a while, but we had a lot of rest stops on the way."

"He says he has a plan for when he gets back, but we don't know what it is," said Nan.

"He said he'd take us to the sea," Tom shouted. "We've never been."

"That might be it," said Edward. "We have good wild seaside in Wales, but I expect Scottish cliffs and waves are even bigger and better." Tom realised he was teasing and decided he liked these Gramps, even though he was still disappointed that their Huffs had not been from Des.

While the grown-ups sat by the fire, resting and chatting over mugs of nettle beer, Emily flew up to Ben's head with Tom to send a Huff to Alice and Ollie. She did it slowly and carefully, but was relieved that Tom couldn't read Huff himself, as she had a feeling there were a few mistakes.

we no hoo maid the huff its are gramps from walez com and see.

"They won't be able to read it," Tom objected, feeling rather left out, even though Emily had read her message aloud for him.

"I bet Old George will be able to read it to them," said Emily. "He knows everything."

Chapter 8

Secrets and Surprises

For the rest of that day, Tom and Emily happily showed their grandparents all round their cave and its surroundings. They took them to the loch to meet the otters, and for Tom to show off his swimming and diving skills. The Gramps paddled but decided they were too tired after their long journey to go swimming. On the way home, the children stopped and made them stand in front of Ben McIlwhinnie, to see if they could spot that here was a real Mountain Giant, not any ordinary hill. To their delight Nan said, "The top of that hill looks exactly like a huge head. It's even got two sticking-out ears!" and they were able to say that she was exactly right.

Although they kept a good lookout for Alice and Ollie, there was no sign of their friends all that day and Emily decided that nobody had managed to read her message after all. But at supper time, Mum said that the family at the camp had agreed to stay away for the day, to give them some time alone with their visitors. Obviously the grown-ups had been doing some signalling of their own, Emily decided, and they had certainly been keeping secrets! They had even cleared a space in the Bone Cave (where Lily's egg had been hidden earlier in the summer) for the Gramps to sleep, and soon after supper they went to bed, tired from their journey.

"Can I go up to Ben to check for Huff?" Emily asked when they had said goodnight and disappeared into the cave.

"Yes, if you're quick. But there's no need to send a Huff to Alice. We're all going down to the camp tomorrow morning. I arranged it with Ellen yesterday."

"You're good at keeping secrets," Tom grumbled. "Can I go up too?"

"No, it's your bedtime. Go and clean your teeth."

Emily grinned happily and flew up to Ben's bald head. She enjoyed being by herself in the gloaming, gazing around the wide stretch of country that surrounded their hill. As she watched, several small deer came out of the woods to drink at the stream before settling down to crop the grass by the water and a large hare shot down the hillside behind her. Almost as fast as flying, she thought as she stood up high to watch as it disappeared over the brow of the hill. The sun was setting and the western sky was a blaze of pink and orange. There were a few clouds streaking the north, grey against the pink, and as she gazed as hard as she could, she thought she saw one shaped like a ring. As she watched, the shape wavered and changed and was lost in the rest of the clouds on the horizon.

"Des," she thought, "one of his smoke rings! It must be." She was so excited that she was about to fly up above the hill, but just then a shout came from below.

"EMILY!"

"In a minute..."

"NOW!"

Emily said a few rude words that she'd learnt from Ollie, but only inside her head. She flew down to the cave.

"Dad, I think I saw a Huff from Des. Like one of his smoke rings. Come up and see. Please!"

"You were imagining things," said her father. "Anyway, it's bedtime."

"Da..ad..."

"If it was Des, he'll come just as fast without a Huff from you," her mother said, coming out of the cave.

"Oh all right," said Emily, "but I'm far too excited to sleep, so there's really no point in going to bed...."

Her parents smiled at each other as she trudged reluctantly into the cave, and sure enough she was asleep almost as soon as her head hit the heather.

When Emily woke next morning her first thought was of Des. She rushed out of her bedroom cave without shaking the heather from her spikes and said breathlessly, "Has he come?"

Everyone else was up. Lily was bouncing and huffing on Nan's knee, Tom and Edward were down at the stream having a wash and Dad was stirring porridge.

"Who?" asked Nan.

"Des, of course!"

"No sign of him," said Mum, bringing the last of their blaeberries to have after the porridge. "You must have been mistaken, Emily. Never mind, we're taking the Gramps to meet our friends today, so you'll have plenty to do without worrying about Des."

"He'll come in his own good time," Nan said comfortingly. "You can never tell when a Traveller will turn up. Come and have breakfast."

Emily felt more cheerful after her breakfast, and they all got ready to fly down to the camp. Tom shot ahead to show them the quickest way, and they landed at the edge of the clearing in the woods.

Suddenly the camp seemed far too full of grown-ups!

Alice and Ollie said a polite hello to Nan and Edward, then the four young dragons looked at each other in unspoken agreement and sidled off towards their tree house.

"They'll be yakking for hours!" said Ollie, and they all agreed. As they landed one by one on the branch, Emily, the last, looked back at the camp.

"Look," she said to Alice. "It's like a rainbow down there!" They both looked. It was true: the blue and green and red and orange of the dragons formed a striped circle round the fire, with the speck of gold that was Lily dancing between them. The boys looked too, and chuckled.

"Yakking is right!" said Tom.

"Old George will like our Gramps," said Emily happily.

They were turning to go though the bracken doorway when Ollie, in the lead, held up a talon and said, "Ssh — listen!"

They could hear a strange noise coming from inside the tree house, a low continuous rumbling.

"What's that?" "Something's in our tree house!" "Someone's pinched it..." They all spoke in whispers and the rumbling went on. Then there was a louder snort. They backed away from the door.

"Shall we get Dad?" Alice whispered.

"Course not!" said Ollie scornfully. "Count of three and we rush in, all together, ready to shoot some flames...."

"NO!" said Emily. "We might set fire to the walls!"

"OK, take it by surprise. Rush in, talons out, no huffing 'til we see what it is. Ready?"

They all nodded.

"GO!"

They crammed through the doorway and there was a crash as Ollie, in the lead, fell over something on the floor. Tom landed on top of him and gave a yell. Emily grabbed Alice before she too fell on the struggling heap, and they stared in amazement at an untidy pile of bundles, heather, pans and dragons on the floor. There was a mighty heave, and Ollie and Tom rolled off in a tangle of tails.

A voice came out of the depths of the heap. "Get lost, you lot! I need some sleep."

"DES!!!"

"Go AWAY!"

"You're back!!"

"SCRAM!!"

"Come on," said Alice. They hauled Tom to his feet, and Ollie followed, wincing and swearing under his breath. They crept through the doorway and tried to pull the bracken closed behind them. Clanks and thuds came to their ears as Des rolled over and settled back to sleep.

Tom scrambled to the end of the branch and yelled down to the camp, "Hey, guess what? Des's back!" Hearing an ominous growl from inside, the others shoved him off the branch and flew after him down to the ground.

"Great!" said Ollie happily, stretching his crumpled wings. "We'll start making plans as soon as he's properly awake."

Chapter 9

Plotting

It was soon obvious that Des would not wake up for a long time. Even Georgie and Lily scampering and squealing round the base of the tree had no effect on the rhythmic snores. Tom and Ollie, who had been chasing them in the hope that their squeaky voices would penetrate Des's dreams, finally admitted defeat.

It was equally obvious that Old George, Nan and Edward could happily talk all day, and though Emily thought a lot of it was interesting, she and Alice soon got restless and kept wondering whether Des was awake.

Finally their mothers took pity on them. "Des will probably sleep for hours," Gwen said. "Why don't you all go off for a fly, and come back for supper? He'll be much more pleased to see you if you let him sleep in peace for a few hours."

"Here's some food," said Ellen, giving them a bag. They took it and went to find the boys, who agreed to go exploring for the rest of the day.

"What we really need is extra flying practice," said Ollie at lunch time. "If we can prove to Des and the Parents that we can fly anywhere without needing lifts all the time they'll HAVE to let us go off with him."

The others were less convinced of this, but they saw his point. Alice and Ollie demonstrated the wing-strengthening exercises that their father had taught them on their many travels, and they stood in a circle giggling and flapping energetically, trying to follow Ollie's moves. Then, for the rest of the afternoon, they practised wheeling, banking, weaving through trees, low-flying dodging of bushes and boulders, emergency braking and, finally, fast bursts of racing speed. Tom was so determined to keep up with the others that he was almost falling out of the sky with weariness by the time Alice called a halt.

They found a stream and slaked their thirst, then realised the sun was beginning to sink.

"We'd better not be late for supper," said Alice. "And surely Des will be awake by now. Tom, are you OK to fly home?"

"Of course I am!" said Tom indignantly. "I'm not a bit tired." The others were not convinced, and even Ollie realised that they needed to fly slowly if Tom was to keep up.

"If even YOU can get back without needing a lift, it will prove we're ALL old enough," he said encouragingly, and to Emily's surprise, Tom managed to fly all the way back to camp. He did not chatter as much as usual, but he refused a lift when Ollie offered and Emily was proud of him as they made the final glide and landed wearily beside the fire.

Ollie immediately dashed to listen at the foot of the tree house.

"I can't hear him," he shouted.

"He's down at the small loch having a wash," Ellen said, bringing a talonful of roots and mushrooms for Oliver to add to the pot on the fire.

"He certainly needed one!" said Oliver chuckling. "He was grey all over — not a rainbow spike in sight! The rest are there too. Why don't you join them for a quick swim before supper?"

"Is Tom all right?" asked Ellen anxiously. "He looks tired out." Tom was stretched out on his front with his nose on the ground, panting. He looked almost asleep. Ollie nudged him with a foot.

"He's OK. He flies really well for his age. He didn't need a lift once all day. Did you, Tom?" He kicked Tom a little harder.

Tom opened his eyes and struggled to his feet. "I'm fine," he said. "Let's go for a swim." He and Ollie set off towards the loch, and the girls saw Ollie give him a High Four when they were almost out of sight.

Ellen looked suspiciously at the girls. "Honestly, we're all fine," Emily said hurriedly. "Do you need any help with supper?"

To their relief, Oliver said they would manage, and Alice and Emily hurried after the boys, hoping they'd got away without suspicion.

"Hmm, they're up to something," Ellen said thoughtfully.

On the bank of the small loch they found all the grandparents sitting in a row watching Gwen and Duncan teaching Lily and Georgie to swim. Georgie could manage a few strokes by himself now, with much spluttering and splashing. Lily was riding on her father's back while he swam in slow circles. They were just in time to see Des surface in the very middle of the loch and the two boys leap on top of him in a fountain of spray. He fought them off and ducked them both, then flew to the bank to shake himself and give the girls a wet hug. "Great to see you," he said.

"That looks better," said Nan. "You're green again! Didn't you wash at all while you were away?"

"Not in Ice Land! The waterfalls are fantastic but too cold, the sea is freezing and then I tried a pool but it was hot!"

"Tell us about Ice Land," Emily begged.

"Over supper, then we can all hear his stories," Old George said. "You two go for a quick splash, then we'll all go back. I think Georgie and Lily have had enough."

"I have anyway!" Duncan said, wading ashore with a protesting Lily. "She's never satisfied." He handed Lily — who was huffing "No, no!" — to Nan and shook the water off his wings.

"Have you had a nice day?" Gwen asked, coming ashore with Georgie. Emily was about to tell her about all the flying practice when Alice pulled her into the water whispering, "Don't say anything 'til we've talked to Des." They joined the boys in the deeper water, and all agreed that they would keep very quiet about their plans until the time seemed right.

They splashed ashore, feeling revived and very hungry, and followed the grown-ups back to the camp.

Chapter 10

The Traveller's Tale

After a huge supper of rabbit and mushroom stew, they all sat round the fire feeling too full to move. Lily had gone to sleep under her mother's wing and even Georgie had stopped bouncing and was looking drowsy. Everyone else was keen to hear about Des's adventures, and they bombarded him with questions.

"Was it far?"

"Did you find any other dragons?"

"Were there any Humans? They didn't ever catch sight of you, did they?"

"Was there really a huge dragon huffing underground?"

"Is it covered with ice and snowing all the time?"

"Is there sea all round it? With huge waves crashing on rocks?"

"Were there fiery mountains?"

"Did you find enough to eat? You were hungry enough for three helpings!"

Des put his wings over his ears and took a huge gulp of nettle beer. "OK, OK, I'll tell you!" he said, and proceeded to describe his long flight over the sea with the Bonxie, the Human ships, big ones and little ones, and the huge beasts under the water which came to the surface and sent fountains of spray into the air. It was obvious that some of his listeners thought this was just Des and his wild travellers' tales, but he insisted it was all true.

"I was really tired by the time I saw land ahead," he continued, "but there it was, high mountains rising out of the sea, and guess what? One was smoking! I flew a bit lower and saw there was a bit of green land near the edge, but no trees to hide in. There were signs of Humans about, so I had to be careful, but I found a cave in the cliff and hid while I had a good long sleep."

He stopped for some more beer, and the young dragons waited impatiently. Tom bounced up and down until Ollie said pointedly that he was as bad as Georgie. Remembering their plans he decided to calm down and behave like a grown-up.

"Even in the middle of the night there's light in the sky — even more than here..." Des continued with his story, telling of the seals, the great flocks of birds and the huffing valley and the smoking black mountain which finally convinced him that there were no dragons living there. He had not intended to confess his sightings by Humans, but the young dragons were so thrilled by his stories that he decided to risk it, and they cheered loudly when he told of the Bonxies' attack on the beach party.

Tom was particularly delighted. "Were they all covered with Bonxie poo? Wicked!"

"Did you help drive them away?" asked Ollie.

"Well, no, obviously not," said Des, with a glance at the grown-ups. "The whole point was to make sure they didn't see me. Bonxies often dive-bomb Humans if they get too near their nests, so I don't suppose they were suspicious at all."

"They had found your cave, though," Duncan said. "And a dog might have sniffed you out if the Bonxies hadn't been there to rescue you."

It was obvious that the grown-ups did not admire Desmond's exploits quite as much as the children did.

"Desmond, you take far too many risks with Humans," said Edward gravely. "You were just the same in Wales. If you get captured we'll all be in danger."

"Yes, we HAVE to stay as storybook creatures," Ellen agreed. "It's the only way we'll survive as free dragons. If Humans realise we still exist they'll search for us and they won't give up easily."

The young dragons could feel their chances of travelling with Des slipping away. Ollie changed the subject.

"How did you get home without that Bonxie?"

"Well, once you know that you can float for a rest it helps a lot."

"That would work on a calm sea," Old George said wisely. "But what if the waves are really high?

I would have thought you'd risk getting your wings swamped. It's been pretty windy lately..."

Des looked sheepish. "Well, I didn't actually fly *all* the way. I hitched a lift on one of those floating houses. It was quite safe..." he insisted, drowning out their cries of horror. "I hadn't planned to, but one loomed out of the dark and nearly ran me over while I was having a float. So I thought, why not? I found a good hiding place under a wee boat on deck where no one could see me and slept most of the way back to Scotland. When we were in sight of one of Ben's islands, I flew off and made my way back here. Honestly, it was as safe as caves!"

"You are hopeless!" Nan said affectionately. "I don't know how you've stayed out of a cage for so long!"

"He's just naturally brilliant, aren't you, Des?" said Emily. Des blushed and took another swig of nettle beer.

"Did you find any good places along the coast on your way home?" Ollie asked, trying to sound casual. The others held their breath.

Des grinned round at them. "As a matter of fact I did!" he said and yawned loudly. "But I'm far too tired to tell you any more tonight. Can I sleep in your tree house again? It's brilliant by the way. I like the bracken door and the decorations on the walls."

Alice and Emily smirked triumphantly at the boys. "Of course you can," said Alice. "We often do, but we can sleep at home for tonight."

"Ollie and me can sleep up there too," said Tom eagerly, but the idea was swiftly vetoed by the others. Nobody liked the idea of the boys making wild plans with Des. This was not the way to convince their parents it was safe to let them go off on a trip with him!

"No chance!" said Des firmly, getting up and swigging the last of his beer. "Goodnight all. Thanks for a great supper. See you in the morning. Or perhaps the afternoon..." He set off towards the tree house.

"I hope he doesn't fall off on the way up!" said Emily, watching his unsteady progress through the trees.

"Des always falls on his feet," said her Gran comfortingly.

Chapter 11

Persuading the Parents

I t was midday when Des reappeared, yawning and stretching, but more like his old self. The youngsters let him enjoy his breakfast and then dragged him up the hill to demonstrate their improved flying techniques and prove to him that they were ready for an adventure.

After a while, Ollie called a halt and they sat in a row on a large flat rock to hear Des's opinion of their flying.

"Pretty good," he said. "Well done, especially you, Tom. OK, I *did* find a nice bit of seaside on my way home. In fact I stayed a couple of days. It's due west of here, wild and rocky, with cliffs and a good cave big enough for all of us to shelter in if we need to. There's enough driftwood and seaweed lying around on the high tide line for a few fires. Plenty of shellfish. Best of all, there was no sign of Humans, and I had flown for quite a way southwards along the coast before I found this bay. If your parents agree, we could go for a few days. How's that?"

"Brilliant!" said Ollie, and the others agreed.

"Let's ask them tonight after dinner," said Emily.

"If we go back early we could help get it ready," said Alice, and they all agreed that was good thinking!

When they got back to camp they discovered that the meal that night was to be outside the cave on Ben McIlwhinnie's ledge, so the youngsters set out to be as helpful as possible, collecting food and jumping firewood. Ollie even offered to take Georgie out of the way for a while, which was so unusual that his mother regarded him suspiciously as he set off for a splash in the stream with his little brother.

"We'd better not overdo it!" Alice whispered to Emily, noticing her mother's look.

They left any talk of expeditions until everyone was full and sitting round the fire feeling rather sleepy. Des had flown up to see if Ben was awake to hear about Ice Land, but he came down to report that he was so deeply asleep that not even a big huff up his nose had any effect. Nan and Edward, who hadn't met him, were disappointed but agreed there was nothing they could do about it.

When Des came back down, all four young dragons glared pointedly at him until he broached the subject of the trip to the sea. He emphasised the loneliness of the place and the total lack of Humans until he had talked himself to a standstill, and they held their breaths anxiously, waiting for the comments of the grown-ups.

"How long would it take to get there?" Oliver started, after a long pause.

"Two days max, and there are plenty of places to camp on the way."

"Could Tom manage the flight?" his mother asked anxiously.

"Mu-um!" Tom protested, but Des shushed him. "I'm sure he could, but I can always give him a lift if he needs one. The others should be fine. I'll take good care of them, I promise."

"Are you sure you can find the place again?" said Duncan.

"Easy. We pick up the little river that flows into the cove and follow it all the way. Can't get lost, honestly."

"Please let us go!" said Emily.

Nan, who had said nothing so far, looked round the group thoughtfully. The four parents were still looking uncertain and Duncan was shaking his head. Ollie was starting to look rebellious and the girls anxious. Tom was scowling. Des sighed, looked round them all and shrugged his wings as if to say "I did my best!" She looked last at Emily, who looked back at her with such a pleading expression that Nan decided to speak.

"Let them go," she said. "I've known Desmond since he was a hatchling. And though he can seem wild and reckless, he really is a clever Traveller, and you can trust him not to take risks if he's in charge of your children. They need to be allowed to try their wings."

"Oh Gran!" cried Emily, and flung her wings round her in delight. Old George was nodding his head in agreement.

"We-ell," said Ellen.

"Thanks Mum!" said Ollie before she could say any more. "I'll help Des look after the others I promise." His parents looked at him sceptically, but Alice said reassuringly, "We'll all be sensible, Mum. We won't take any risks."

Emily and Tom looked pleadingly at their parents.

Edward saw that they were still a little anxious. "I have an idea," he said. "Nan and I have to start for home soon. Why don't we fly west with them until they reach this cove that Des has found, and then head south for Wales from there? Then we can make sure they reach it safely and it's not too far for Tom. What do you say?"

"Fine by me," said Des. "It will be great to have some good stories round the campfire at night." Edward was famous for his storytelling.

"That would help," said Gwen, relieved. "Duncan?"

There was a long pause and Emily and Tom fixed their Dad with pleading stares. "All right, you can go," said Duncan finally, and smiled as the four children erupted into whoops and cheers of delight.

"Don't wake Georgie and Lily!" Gwen said. "They'll want to go too!"

Chapter 12

The Secret Cove

It was a fine morning two days later when the seven dragons, carrying enough food for the journey, took off and headed west, their families waving until they were out of sight. Ollie gave a great huff of relief. "I thought they'd NEVER let us away," he whooped.

"Thanks to our Gramps," Emily reminded him, and Ollie grinned and attempted a High Four with her in mid air.

Now that Tom had got his own way, he was less reluctant to accept the occasional lift from Des, so they made good time and were well on their way to the coast before they stopped to camp for the night.

After supper, Edward told them a story. He was an excellent storyteller, and even Des was held spellbound by the old tale of the famous Red Dragon of Wales, who was afraid of nothing, not even Humans. "In fact, the Humans thought he was so great that they even put a picture of him on their flags! It doesn't look like him at all, but it shows how famous he was," he finished, and everybody applauded and begged for just one more story. Instead Nan began to sing an old Welsh ballad, and they all joined in the chorus until the song ended with a quiet verse that made them all feel sleepy enough to curl up in the bracken round the fire and gradually fall asleep.

They caught their first sight of the sea the next afternoon, flying high and close together for safety. To their delight they could see shadowy shapes of islands in the distance, and even a boat, which Des recognised as the same shape as the one he'd hitched a lift on. But the land below was still wild and seemed empty of roads or any sign of Humans. Des spotted the white thread of the stream he wanted to follow, and led them in a line, with Edward coming last, until it passed through a series of marshy pools and finally tumbled over rocks and onto the shore.

They were there! Tired but triumphant, they soared down to land among the rocks at the back of a small semi-circle of sandy beach, backed by high cliffs.

Ollie stared at the sea lapping on the sand. "That doesn't look very wild!" he said. "I thought you said all the sea in Scotland was rough, Des. I've seen bigger waves down south."

"It's lucky for us it's so calm," said Nan. "We've had very good weather for our flight. It would have taken a lot longer if we'd had the west wind against us. How about a paddle?"

"We must check for Humans first," warned Edward. "You can't be too careful on a beach. They seem to like the seaside for some reason, especially the little ones. Stay by these rocks, and be ready to fly if we shout." He and Des flew cautiously round the back of the little beach, checked inside the cave they could see on the far side, and finally came back to them.

"NOW can we go in the sea?" cried Tom, dancing with impatience, and Edward finally agreed it was safe. Huffing with delight, the four of them raced each other to the water's edge and threw themselves into the sea, splashing and spluttering. Des flew over them and dived into the deeper water. Nan and Edward sat on the rocks and laughed at the sight of the coloured wings and spiky tails reappearing in a tangle of foam. Several seagulls flew up from the water in alarm, and a flock of smaller birds at the water's edge ran away as fast as they could.

"I have a feeling we're disturbing the peace," said Nan. "Let's check out the cave and build a fire. They'll be chilly when they come out."

"And hungry!" laughed Edward. "Let's collect some seaweed. I bet the kids have never tasted crispy fried seaweed."

"And we can show them how you knock limpets off rocks with your tail. They don't have shellfish in the mountains!"

By the time the youngsters had splashed themselves to a standstill and then spread their wings and danced on the beach in the sun to get warm again, supper was cooking on a fire outside the cave and the sun was sinking behind a bank of cloud on the horizon. Nan and Edward were heating up the last of the food they had brought with them, and there was just enough to go round. All the youngsters were suspicious of the seaweed that had been crisped in the fire, but agreed to try some.

"Makes a great snack," said Des, crunching heartily. "You can crisp it with Huff if you haven't time to light a fire. It's saved my life many a time."

"But you'll need to go foraging tomorrow," Edward said. "Make sure you check with Des if you don't know what you're picking."

"He hasn't poisoned himself yet!" Nan laughed, but Des looked a bit sheepish, remembering several times when he had made himself rather sick. He decided to change the subject.

"What else do you want to do tomorrow?" he asked.

Edward and Nan looked at each other. "I think we should start for home," Edward said. "It's a long way and we need to take it in stages. Now we know you can travel safely, we should go, Nan."

"Oh Gran!" protested Emily. "Why can't you stay?"

"We'll have no one to tell us a story at bedtime," said Alice, who had become fond of Emily's grandparents too.

"Time for a last one now, if you like," said Edward.

Nan looked across at Emily. "You tell your story, but I think I'd like a stroll. Why don't you come with me, Emily?"

Emily jumped up and she and Nan strolled down the beach and along the water's edge, until they came to a high rock at the end of the bay. A quick flap of their wings and they were on the top with a lovely view of the sunset reflected in the calm sea. They settled down close together.

"Gran, why can't you stay with us?" Emily said with a little quiver in her voice. "I don't know when we'll see you again."

Nan put a wing round her. "Oh, I don't think it will be too long. Think how much you have done this year, Emily. All those ideas you had, finding your new cave, and Des and Alice and the others. I'm really proud of you! I came expecting a little girl dragon, and I find you're growing up. I don't think it will be too long before *you* are flying to Wales to visit *us*."

"But I don't know if Alice will be staying for the winter. And Des will go off travelling again. It'll be awful without them. What shall I do, all on my own?"

"Winter is a good time for thinking and reading and planning," her Gran said. "Don't waste it. You won't lose Alice or Des or me forever. Keep practising your Huff! Look at the sky — isn't it beautiful?"

They sat together in silence, staring over the sea, and Emily felt happier with Gran's words "I'm really proud of you" ringing in her head. Suddenly a voice came from the beach below. "Are you two planning to sleep up there? Tom's flat out and the rest of them want to kip. I'm going for a nightfly, but I'll creep back quietly."

"All right Des, we're coming!" Nan called. "He never seems to get tired — unless he's flown all the way from Ice Land," she added chuckling as they made their way back to the cave and settled down to sleep with the others in the glow of the dying fire.

Chapter 13

The Warning Huff

When Emily woke next morning the sun was up but the sea was a good deal rougher and a brisk wind was blowing. The others were still stretched out on the soft sand fast asleep, but Edward was reviving the fire, and Nan was walking slowly along the tide-line collecting things. Emily got up and stretched, then ran down to her.

"I'm collecting cockles and mussels for breakfast," Nan said as Emily reached her. Emily had never seen shellfish before, but she soon found that there were lots lying on the beach and in the shallow water, though many were empty shells.

"I hope this will be enough for our breakfast," she said, rather worried, but at that moment, Des came up behind them.

"Fantastic!" he said. "Fish!"

"Where?"

"Out there. Look at the birds." Des pointed to the bay where a large flock of seagulls were wheeling and diving just off shore and then took off towards them. He flew straight into the middle of the flock, scattering birds, and dived. Emily danced with excitement as he came soaring back, dropped a fish at her feet and headed back. Nan was just in time to catch the fish before it flapped back into the water.

"Take this to Edward," she said to Emily, "and see if the others are awake enough to help."

They were all awake, and Ollie immediately took off to help Des with the fishing. Alice and Emily relayed the fish they dropped back to the fire, while Tom danced and yelled encouragement until Ollie dropped a flapping mackerel on his head. Finally Nan said they had enough and told Tom to wash the fish-scales off in the sea before breakfast.

"How did you know there would be fish out there?" Emily asked Des when he and Ollie flew back with their last two fish and shook the seawater from their wings. Tom scowled and swung his tail at Ollie in revenge, but Ollie just laughed and dodged. Nan sympathised and gave Tom the first of the sizzling fish to keep him quiet.

"You can tell whenever you see a big flock of gulls just off shore. They've found a shoal of fish in fairly shallow water. Mind you, I wouldn't go out if there were Bonxies in the flock. And you need to watch out for Gannets too. They have beaks that could take your tail off! If it's just seagulls it's fine."

"I don't think you'll go hungry with Des around," said Edward, threading the last of the little fish onto the stick over the fire. "Now, how far south did you fly from here, Des? Will Nan and I be safe if we follow the coast, or would we be better inland? We must make sure no Humans see us."

Des looked sheepish and mumbled something through his mouthful of fish. Nan looked at him suspiciously. "You did check out the area to the south, didn't you? You told Gwen and the others that the place was safe."

"Yes, well, I'm pretty sure it is. I know it's safe to the north because that's the way I came, and I did fly up the hill back there and look south and it seemed OK, and I haven't seen any sign of Humans so far, so I thought...."

"You thought you'd risk it!" Edward sounded annoyed. "Well that's fine when you're on your own, but you did tell their parents it was safe. I don't think they would have been happy if they'd known you hadn't checked properly."

"Well we're here now," said Ollie cheerfully. "Not much they can do about it."

"Shut up, Ollie," said Alice, who was afraid Edward would send them straight back home. "Why don't we promise to stay around here today, and you can send us a Huff this evening telling us whether it's safe to do a bit of exploring?"

"That's very sensible, Alice," said Nan. "Do you all promise? No crossed tails!" Everyone nodded solemnly. She glared at Des until he nodded agreement too. "Good. Then I think we should make a start, Edward. We'll get as far as we can before Gloaming Huff time."

They all flew to the top of the cliff to wave goodbye. Nan hugged them all, with a specially big hug and huff for Emily, Edward clapped wings and reminded Des to have some sense of responsibility for a change, then the two elderly dragons took off and soared away south. The others waved their wings until they were out of sight. Alice looked at Emily, who was looking a little tearful, and decided to be organising.

"Right, you three can start looking for food up here. We need more than shellfish and seaweed. Emily and I are going back to the beach. Don't get lost. Are you sad to see your Gran go?" she asked Emily as they flew back to the cave.

Emily landed and heaved a sad sigh. "I don't know whether I'll see them again. They're getting quite old, and it's a long way to Wales. Gran said she thought I could visit *them*, but I can't 'til I'm older. And I wouldn't be allowed to go by myself." She sniffed back tears.

"I'll come with you, just as soon as we can," said Alice comfortingly. "Come on, there's a big rock pool over there. There might be some shrimps and crabs for supper."

The boys came back with food and firewood, and after lunch they all jumped waves, which were higher now and breaking on the beach with a satisfying roar. Des showed them how to lie flat on their stomachs and ride the waves as they came in, and they all tried it, shrieking with laughter as they tumbled in the shallows. By evening they were tired, and ready to gather round the fire for supper, but Emily reminded Des about the Huff and the two of them went up the hill to watch for the smoke while the others cooked.

It was quite late when the first signal appeared and Emily was getting worried despite Des's reassurances.

good flight and both fine but had to dodge human settlements be careful and don't go near the shiny road are you all ok

"Say we're fine," said Emily, cheering up. Des sat up straight, nose pointing to the sky. "I'm asking what this shiny road is," he said between Huffs.

we don't know just keep away goodnight sleep well

Emily Huffed her own goodnight, adding a row of kisses and then she and Des flew down to the cave.

In the firelight they huddled close and discussed the message in hushed whispers. Des was determined to find out what the mysterious Shiny Road was. "It can't be far away if Nan and Edward found it today. If I go early I can get back and tell you about it. I know how to keep out of sight — I've had lots of practice."

"You needn't think I'm staying behind!" Ollie declared.

"Or me!" said Tom.

"I'd like to know what a shiny road is, as long as we're careful," Emily admitted.

Everyone looked at Alice. "All right, if that's what you all want to do," she agreed reluctantly.

"YESS!" shouted Ollie.

"Right," said Des, "early bed everyone. I'll keep watch and wake you all at dawn."

Chapter 14

Huffs, Clanks and Humans

I n fact it was Alice who woke at dawn, after rather a restless night. She woke the others and they all gathered round the snoring Des.

"Shall I give him a kick?"

"Water on his head?"

"Tail prod?"

Des opened one eye. "Shut up you lot," he mumbled and turned over sleepily.

"IT'S DAWN!" they shouted in unison and Des shot to his feet, scattering sand. "OK, OK, I just dozed off... Gimme some breakfast..."

After breakfast, Des became serious and Alice realised with relief that he was not taking the exploration lightly.

"Right, this Shiny Road will probably be something to do with Humans and could well be very dangerous. If we find it you must all do *exactly* as I say, straight away, no arguing. If anything happens to me, Alice takes charge..."

"Why not me? I'm older and stronger!" Ollie protested.

"Because she's sensible, you're not. And I said no arguing. Any more and you stay behind! Alice, you get them back here, hide and wait and if I don't come back tomorrow, start for home. Keep together. Emily, use the Huff — your parents will be watching out for it. Understand?"

Everyone nodded, looking serious. Even Tom was subdued. In fact he looked rather scared, Emily thought, but she knew he wouldn't agree to stay behind. They had to keep together. It was still quite early and a cloudy morning, though not raining. Des said that was better for reconnaissance than bright sunshine, and led the way up the cliff in single file, Alice bringing up the rear. There was a beaten path running along the cliff edge, but nothing was moving along it, so they crossed and left it behind.

The land on top of the cliff looked flat at first, but they soon realised that there were hummocks and hollows and scattered rocks, so they crept along, keeping low and sometimes stopping and hiding leaving Des to check all around from the top of a rock. They saw no sign of anything like a Shiny Road, or Humans, and they were all starting to relax when Ollie, who was about to argue that he was fed up with crawling and they might as well fly, gave a gasp and pointed south.

"Huff!" he exclaimed. They all swung round and stared. Sure enough, a distinct column of white smoke was rising into the air. "Hey, there must be dragons here! Let's go and find them." He crouched ready to launch himself into the air but Des pulled him back.

"Listen!" he ordered, and then they heard it: a clear "huff...huff" coming nearer and accompanied by a clanking rattle. As they held their breath and huddled closer there was a screech, a whistle and a long sigh. Then silence.

"It's gone," said Ollie, preparing to leave their sheltering rock, but Des shook his head. "I don't know what it was — never heard anything quite like it before — but it's still there. I'm going to try to get nearer and see what it is. You lot stay here. Promise, Ollie?"

Ollie agreed, reluctantly, and they all watched as Des half crept, half flew up the hillock ahead and disappeared. It seemed a very long time until the shape of him reappeared and he came to rejoin them.

"Could you see what it was?" Tom asked eagerly.

"I could see it, but I've no idea what it is," Des answered. "The bad news is that it's a Human beast, and the good news is it's further away than we thought from the sound of it. Remember those fast Human things that run along roads? We saw some near Safari Park. Well it's a bit like that, but long and thin. There were a few Humans climbing out of it, but as I say, they're a good way off, and can't see us from there. I think it must be on the Shiny Road — I could see something silvery running away from it. We need to decide what to do, but no need to worry as long as we don't go too close."

"Let's head the other way to explore. We haven't been that way yet," suggested Alice.

"Typical!" Ollie scoffed. "This is the most interesting thing that's happened so far and you want to go the other way! Don't you want to see what it is?"

But before a row could break out, the strange noise came again: the huffs, the clanks, an even louder whistle, more puffs of smoke and whatever-it-was clanked away into the distance. They waited in tense silence until the sound died away.

"I think we'd better get back to our beach in case it comes again," said Emily, and to her surprise, Des agreed. "Yeah, better there than up here. We can hide in the cave if we need to." He started to lead the way, until Alice said, "Sshh! Listen!"

They froze, flattening themselves into the grass. Clearly through the noise of the rising wind and the distant waves came the sound of Human voices, and they were not far away! They crept forward in a line and peered through the tufts of grass.

Coming along the cliff path was a Human family, dressed in bright clothes; two big ones, and three smaller ones running ahead. It seemed to take them a long time to pass, as they stopped to look at flowers, stare and point across the sea, zigzag to and fro and call loudly to each other as they went. It looked as though they would soon be out of sight but suddenly there was a loud shout of triumph from the leading child and the whole party disappeared down the cliff.

"Oh no!" said Alice. "They've found the path by the stream. They're going to our beach. What are we going to do now?"

"I know what we *can't* do — go back to the beach while they're there! But no need to worry — there's only our fireplace and a few fish bones, and anything could have left those. We'll stay up here until they go. I don't suppose they'll stay long."

"There's not much to do up here," grumbled Ollie. "I vote we sneak up to have a look at that Shiny Road while the Huffer thing isn't there. We can always fly away if we hear it coming back."

Emily looked at Des, realising that he was longing to go and investigate too. It was obvious that he was finding the responsibility of the four of them a bit of a drag.

"Yes, let's go," she said. "It shouldn't be too dangerous. OK Alice?" Alice nodded doubtfully, but it was clear that Tom was all for the idea. Des and Ollie beamed, and they all crept up the side of the hill that led to the Shiny Road. At the top they lay flat in a row and gazed around. Below them, at the end of a shallow valley, they could see a small rectangular building with a glinting metal track leading away from it into the distance. There were no Humans there, but far in the distance, a line of bright specks could be seen heading away over the hill.

"More Humans!" said Alice, pointing a claw.

"Yes, but too far away to see us," said Des. "I think it would be safe enough if I went down to have a quick look. You lot stay here."

"No chance!" said Ollie. "I'm fed up with hanging about. It's obvious there's no one there. I'm coming down with you."

"Me too!" said Tom enthusiastically. Des sighed, obviously too fed up to argue, and the three took off down the hill towards the building. Alice raised her eyebrows at Emily, mouthed "Boys!" and they followed.

There wasn't much to see. The Shiny Road was made of metal and glinted in the sun, and the building was beside it, open on one side. The only sign of Humans was a printed notice fastened to one wall and some crinkly paper blowing around.

"Right, Emily! Reading needed," said Des, pointing to the notice, but it was very disappointing to Alice and Emily as they looked at it together. "Just a list of numbers," said Alice.

"More writing here!" said Ollie from outside. Emily read the word "Inschnamurchan Steam Railway Terminus" in faded red letters across the front of the building.

"A railway!" she said. "That comes into some stories I've read. Humans go on holidays in carriages pulled by an engine. I never thought I'd see one for myself!"

"I thought they would be bigger than this," said Alice.

"Obviously this is just a little one!" said Ollie. "I vote we hide in those bushes over there by the track and see if the Huffer thing comes back."

"The train," Emily corrected him.

"Whatever. Go on, Des, you know you want to see it too!"

Des hesitated. "Well, I suppose you can hear it coming quite a way off. OK, you stay here, find a good place to hide and make sure you're well hidden if the train comes back. Remember, it's the *Humans* on the train that are dangerous."

"Aren't you staying?" asked Alice.

"I want to go back to the cliff to see if those Humans are still on our beach," said Des. "Anyone coming with me?"

"I will," said Emily. "This place isn't very interesting." Secretly she thought the Human family looked just like some of the pictures of people in her stories and she was longing for a closer look.

"OK, Alice you stay and make sure Ollie and Tom don't do anything stupid," Des ordered. He pretended he didn't hear Ollie's snort of disgust as he and Emily took off.

Chapter 15

Prints in the Sand

I t did not take long for Des and Emily to fly back to the top of the cliff above their cave. They landed to listen. Clear above the pounding of the waves were the sounds of shrieks and shouts. Des groaned.

"Still there!" he said. "Let's risk a peep over the edge." They crawled cautiously to the rocky cliff edge and peered over. They were directly above their cave and the remains of their camp fire and Emily gasped. "Des, look! They'll see that and know we were there, and they'll come looking for us."

Clearly marked in the soft sand at the edge of the cave were the outlines of five dragons! Emily could make out the shapes of bodies, wings and tails. Some were blurred where the dragons had stirred in their sleep, but there was enough left to make Humans suspicious. The long spiky tails, some straight, some curled, were especially clear.

"The sea doesn't reach there. I never thought of prints in the sand," Des admitted. "But don't worry, they won't have seen it — look, they're over by the water."

"I can see Human footprints near them, and two are coming this way," Emily pointed out. Sure enough, a girl in a green jersey and rolled up jeans was dragging a bigger Human towards the cave. The dragons could hear their voices clearly from the top of the cliff.

"Dad, look, something's had a fire here, and LOOK! Look at the shapes!" The girl pointed and then shouted down the beach, "David, Sam, come and see this..." The two smaller figures came running across from the water's edge, with a bigger one following behind. The girl in green danced with excitement. "Be careful you don't smudge them. Now look. What does that remind you of?"

The five Humans gathered around and gazed at the sandy patch. "Someone's been drawing in the sand, that's all," said the biggest.

"It's monsters!" said the smallest.

"Naa! Aliens!"

"Look at the SHAPE!" said the girl excitedly. "It's a tail with a spike. Here's another! There were more, but you've smudged them. Here's a claw and here's a wing. It's a dragon! There were dragons here, sleeping on the sand. They've made a fire too."

Emily and Des heard the sound of laughter. "What an imagination! You've been reading too many fantasy books."

"We're not likely to find dragons, even in the wilds of Scotland! Must be seals."

"Dragons aren't real, are they Mum?" The smallest sounded a little anxious.

"Of course not! Come on, Phoebe, say goodbye to your imaginary dragons, it's nearly time to get the next train back. You're all rather wet, and it's a bit too chilly to wait for the last one."

"Oh Mu..um...!"

"Come on, daftie! Honestly, dragons...!!"

The five of them set out across the curve of the beach towards the path on the far side. The girl lagged behind and Emily saw her bending and marking the sand as she passed. Then she ran to catch up with her family and they saw a friendly argument break out between the children as they disappeared; laughter and shouts of "Was!" "Wasn't!" floated on the wind.

Des nudged Emily. "We'd better move away a bit," he murmured in her ear. "They'll be coming back along the path." They hid behind a large boulder and soon heard the babble of voices and laughter pass and fade away.

Emily beamed with happiness. "That was magic!" she said. "I've always wanted to see a real Human family. And that girl actually believed in dragons! I do wish I could have let her see me so that she'd know we were real."

"Much too dangerous," warned Des. "I only hope Alice has got the boys into hiding. We can't fly over to warn them with those people in the way. If you ask me, we've had a narrow escape. We'd better smooth out that sandy patch before we leave."

Emily looked back towards the beach and sighed. "I think I would have liked that girl. Oh, look Des! Look what's she's written for me!"

Down on the hard sand was a clear message in large capital letters:

HI DRAGONS!

"Wait 'til Alice sees that!" said Emily happily as they made their way cautiously back to the little railway to find the others.

Chapter 16

The Final Wave

Back at the railway station, the boys and Alice were having a much less interesting time. There really was very little to see around the station and although the clump of bushes that Ollie had spotted was full of interesting berries and some large snails, only Alice was keen on foraging for their supper. Ollie and Tom followed the curve of the railway track a little way, but there was no sign of the train returning, and the line of Humans they had spotted had disappeared over the hill.

Ollie was just starting to argue that they should go back to their beach and scare the Humans away when the faint train whistle was heard in the distance. They crept along the line of bushes until they were quite close to the track but some distance from the station.

Then they waited. The little steam engine, pulling five covered carriages, came huffing down the track, sounding very loud to the crouching dragons. Suddenly it let out its piercing whistle. Alice shut her eyes tightly and put her wings over her ears as it passed, going quite slowly as it got nearer to the station. Then she heard Tom gasp, "Ollie!" and realised that her reckless brother had flown after the departing train, caught up with it, and was riding on the roof of the last carriage, lying flat and almost hidden by the decorative edging on the roof. He looked back and clasped his wings triumphantly above his head grinning at them. Alice was horrified and Tom was furious. "He could have taken me with him!" he fumed.

The train rounded the curve and Alice and Tom hurried after it as fast as they could. They were just in time to see Ollie slide backwards off the roof and dive into the shelter of the bushes as the train came to a halt with a burst of steam from its funnel. This time only one Human got out. He climbed from the front, stretched and disappeared inside the station.

"Ollie, that was SO stupid! Whatever will Des say? He'll never agree to take us anywhere ever again," Alice panted as she reached Ollie, who High-Foured an admiring Tom.

"No danger, nobody could see me up there. I didn't go near a window. I'd like to go for a proper ride. We could all go. A carriage each. I'll ask Des when he gets back. I bet he's never ridden a train before." Ollie was smirking and full of himself, and obviously quite determined to repeat his performance as soon as the train moved off. It was equally obvious that Tom would want to go too. Alice wished that Des would come back and take over. She decided that being left in charge had its drawbacks!

As they argued, voices were heard. They peered through the leaves and saw the five Humans from the beach running along the path towards the station. One of the children turned and pointed towards two large seagulls flying past. "Look Phoebe — dragons!" he shouted and the girl punched him indignantly. The two grown-ups climbed into a carriage while the children went to watch the engine shunt past the carriages and attach itself to the other end of the train. The boys watched too, but Alice had heard what they said.

"You don't think they found Des and Emily do you?" she worried. "Why else would they mention dragons? Oh, I wish they'd come back!"

Ollie suddenly became more responsible. "Those were the Humans who went down to our beach, so now they're safely back here we could go and look for them if you like."

"No need," said Tom. "Here they come." His sharp eyes had spotted two crawling figures making their way cautiously towards the bushes.

"Oh, thank goodness you're back!" said Alice.

"Guess what!" Emily and Tom said together, but Tom's voice was louder. "Ollie rode on the train! Honestly! On the roof..."

Ollie looked a little anxiously at Des. "No Human could see, honestly. I jumped on from behind and lay flat on the roof, then I slid off just before it stopped. Dead easy!"

"What did it feel like?" Des asked, and Alice could see that he was more admiring than angry.

122

"Shoogly! I could feel the shakes through my tummy. But it wasn't going very fast, of course. Let's all have a go. Look, five carriages, one each, and it might go for miles, really fast. No-one will see us, and we can fly off the back any time we like. Please, Des. You know you want to!"

It was obvious to them all that Des did! Alice sighed, and looked to Emily for support.

"They already know about us," Emily warned, but Des said, "Only one of the little ones. The rest didn't believe her." And she knew he wanted to ride the train whatever the risks.

They all jumped as the train's whistle sounded.

"Quick, get ready to jump when it starts off!" Ollie said. "Alice, Emily, you coming?"

"Yes!"

"I suppose we'd better go, to keep an eye on them," Alice said, and Emily beamed.

Des took charge. "Ollie first, to show how it's done; Tom next, then Emily, then Alice, me last. When I decide we need to get off, I'll pass the message along and we all fly down, being careful not to fly past the windows. Clear?" They all nodded as the engine started to huff steam into the air and slowly began to move. As it passed them, Emily saw her family looking out of the window of the second carriage towards the sea, away from them. She wished the girl had been looking her way. Three more Humans had arrived and climbed into another carriage, but there was no sign of the big group returning from the hills. She hoped they would be safe, but was too excited to be really worried.

As the carriages steamed past them, Des gave the signal and Ollie took off and landed on the first carriage roof. Tom followed close, landing with rather a bump on the second. Then Emily found herself flying over the carriages, faster than the train, even though it was gathering speed. She landed safely and looked back to see Alice arriving and Des airborne. As soon as they were all safe she turned back to watch the way they were going.

The train, going faster now, was just as shoogly as Ollie had said, and the vibrations seemed to shake her all over. She found herself giggling quietly and looking round, saw that Alice was enjoying the ride as well. Then she looked ahead to where Tom was crouching on the second carriage and gasped with horror. He had forgotten about his tail! His long blue tail, with its spiky end, was hanging down in full view of the window. And inside that carriage was the family from the beach.

"Tom! Your tail!" she whispered as loudly as she dared.

Tom turned his head. "What?"

"Your TAIL!" This time he heard her, and whisked it out of sight.

Holding her breath, she heard, faintly through the window of his carriage, the voice of the girl from the beach. "I SAID something had landed on the roof and just now I saw something long and blue like a tail. It's gone now." "Ha, ha! I bet it had a spiky end too..." "I didn't have time to see properly." "There's nothing there. Look, we can see the seals on the beach this side."

They were passing a patch of tangled woodland on the landward side of the track and the train seemed to be slowing down. Emily felt a tug from

Alice on her own tail and saw that Des was signalling to them to fly down. She passed the tug to Tom and got ready. One by one they turned round carefully to face the back of the train, and followed Des as he launched himself off the end of the last carriage and landed among the trees.

They were just in time. They heard a loud whistle and the train rounded a bend and slid to a stop at another station. Human voices and the banging of carriage doors could be heard beyond the trees above the huffing of the engine.

"Tom, that girl saw your tail!"

"She couldn't have."

"She did! I heard her tell the others."

"Well I bet they didn't believe her," said Ollie and the rest chorused, "Everybody knows dragons don't exist!"

Emily felt slightly annoyed. Her girl HAD believed in dragons. She crawled a little way from the others and reached a gap in the trees. Peering through she saw the train just beginning to move away and there was the girl looking out of her window. Everyone else on the train

127

seemed to be looking the other way. Emily glanced back to check that none of her friends was looking at her, then stood up as tall as she could and waved a wing at the girl.

She saw the girl's mouth open in surprise and then she was smiling and waving too as the train huffed out of sight. Emily smiled to herself as Des called softly "Emily, we're going back to the cave!" She joined the others and they all flew up together. It would be her secret!

As they got nearer to their beach, she remembered the message in the sand and told Alice to look down as they flew over it. They were just in time to see the last of the words "HI DRAGONS" disappear under the waves of the incoming tide.

"Just as well," said Des comfortingly, as Emily gave a disappointed wail. "The message was only for you. You wouldn't want anyone else seeing it."

"I did see it, just before it disappeared," whispered Alice.

"What are you two on about?" said Ollie landing with a flurry of sand, and Emily and Alice smiled at each other, sharing the secret.

"That was great, riding that train!" Ollie continued, without waiting for an answer, as they arrived at the entrance to their cave. "Can we go back tomorrow for a longer one, Des?"

"Wait 'til we tell the parents!" crowed Tom.

"I think we should be rather careful about that," said Des. "We've been very lucky. If I had known there were so many Humans around this bit of coast I'd never have brought you. You can't be too careful where Humans are concerned..." He stopped as all four burst into derisive laughter at the idea of Des EVER remembering to be careful.

"OK, OK!" he said laughing with them. "But we're heading for home tomorrow so remember, not a word, or you might be banned from travelling ever again. And we've a few marks in the sand to rub out before we go."

"And we could take a bag of seaweed home for everybody," Alice suggested.

"You can collect it then! Slimy stuff!" Ollie shuddered. "Those mussels were OK though."

"Do we HAVE to go home tomorrow?" Tom protested, but to his surprise, Ollie agreed with Des.

"If that and yukky seaweed is all there is for supper," he said, pointing to the very small pile of snails and berries that Alice had foraged in the bushes, "I vote we start right now!"

"I DID see a dragon from the train," the girl said dreamily. Her parents and brothers left the seaside window and sat down as the train rattled along. "Just a little one..."

"Was it a red one? A green one? Breathing fire?" the older brother scoffed.

"No it was a lovely purply-blue, it had lighter wings and I think the spikes on its back were pink and green. It didn't breathe fire. It was friendly. It waved to me..."

Her parents looked at each other and smiled.

END OF BOOK THREE

Things are tense in the Highland glen as winter approaches. An unwelcome visitor makes Ollie rebel.

He runs away but there's a risk he'll be found by Humans. The Dragons set out on a search and rescue mission, full of danger and excitement.
With Des away, it's Emily and Alice to the rescue!

Share their adventures in *Dragon Tales Book IV: The Runaway* by Judy Hayman, coming soon.

APPENDIX
Bonxies and Bonxie Language

"Bonxie" is the name given to the Great Skua in the Highlands and Islands of Scotland. It is a good nickname, as Great Skuas are large and powerful seabirds, fond of terrorising smaller birds and stealing food from them, and attacking any Humans who chance to stray too near their nests. They are dark brown, with strong beaks and a wide wing-span. They nest on the ground, especially on islands, but travel for miles over the sea for fishing.

I once had a narrow escape from nesting Bonxies on the island of Hoy. They missed, fortunately (unlike the ones that attacked the Humans investigating Des's cave!).

The Bonxie who helps Des in this story speaks in a Scottish dialect, and you may need some help understanding him.

If you read the words aloud you will probably guess what they mean — it's just the spelling and missing letters that makes the words look different. But some words have a particular meaning in Scots. Here are some you will find in this book and in the earlier books in this series. (The otters in the loch speak Scots too.)

Loch: a freshwater lake, like the one near the Dragons' cave. (A little one is a 'lochan'.)

Gloaming: evening, twilight or dusk. (Very important for Dragons because it's the time of the Gloaming Huff.)

Bairns: children

Blaeberries: the Scots name for blueberries — or bilberries or whinberries in different parts of England

Selkies: seals (There are a lot of lovely old tales about Selkies told in Scotland.)

Dreich: dark, drizzly, miserable weather. (Wonderful Scots word to describe a wet Highland day!)

Drookit: soaked with water

Birled: whirled

Feart: frightened

Bidin': living

Guddle: muddle

Ken: know ('ye ken' is used exactly like 'you know')

Yin: one

Keek: look

Heid: head, or chief

Frae: from

Mair: more

Gae: Go

Thirz: there's or there are

Afore: before

Onyways: anyway

Dinnae: don't

Dinnae fash: don't worry

Isnae: isn't

Nae: No

Naebdy: nobody

Nae danger: no problem or no chance

Acknowledgements

Heartfelt thanks to all the members of my family, as always; this time especially Rachel and Kate, marketing supremos; David, for inspiring the cover illustration and Megan for a stream of good ideas.

To my fantastic and talented partners in this book project, Caroline and Alison.

To Gordon and Margaret, experts in Bonxie language; George, for advice on foraging and wild living; Ettie; Kitty; Rosie and Isla; Trina, Claire, and the staff of Haddington Library.

And to all the children in the schools I have visited, for their lively ideas and enthusiasm for reading, writing and dragons; and the teachers who organised visits and welcomed me to their classrooms. Special thanks to Mrs Woodward and the children of the Shaftoe Trust School in Heydon Bridge, Northumberland.

About the Author

Judy Hayman lives with her husband Peter on the edge of the Lammermuir Hills in East Lothian, Scotland, where there is a wonderful view and plenty of wildlife, but no dragons, as far as she knows. At various times in her past life she has taught English in a big comprehensive school; written plays, directed and occasionally acted for amateur theatre companies; been a Parliamentary candidate for both Westminster and the Scottish Parliament; and a Mum. Sometimes all at once. Now preventing the Lammermuirs from taking over her garden, being a Gran, writing more Dragon Tales and visiting schools to talk about them takes up a lot of her time.

About the Illustrator

Caroline Wolfe Murray studied Archaeology at the University of Edinburgh and took a career path in the field, turning her hand to archaeological illustration. She has always had a passion for exploration and discovery which evolved from her experience of living in Spain, Belgium, Venezuela and New Zealand. She now resides in East Lothian with her husband James and her two young daughters Lily and Mabel, who have been her inspiration to work on a children's book.

Read on for the first chapter of Dragon Tales Book IV: The Runaway, *coming soon...*

Chapter 1

Secret Plans

Tom and Ollie were hiding in their tree house. It was a bit of a ramshackle affair, just a small shoogly platform and a screen of pine branches wedged into the fork of an elderly oak. It had only one advantage: nobody else ever wanted to sit in it.

If they peered through the gaps in the walls they could just see another tree house — a much more splendid creation. That one had taken many days to build, and everyone had helped, even the grown-ups. It was halfway up the biggest oak in their patch of woodland and not too close to the camp by the loch that Ollie's family had set up in the early summer. It had a proper floor, and walls with windows and a flat branch for landing on, so you could fly up and enter without an undignified scramble through the branches.

Unfortunately it also belonged to the girls!

While the building was in progress, the four young dragons had worked together quite well. On fine days, Tom and his older sister Emily had flown over from their cave on the hill and they had worked hard at the building. On wet days Ollie and Alice had visited the cave, and they had drawn elaborate plans on smooth bits of Emily's bedroom wall. There had been a good deal of arguing of course, but no real fights. In the cave, Ollie and Tom could always move into Tom's room, to make wild plans of their own, but in the finished tree house, there was nowhere to plan in secret.

The four had spent most of the morning arguing about whose turn it was to fetch fresh heather for seats and beds, and finally the boys had left and hidden up their own tree, feeling thoroughly fed up.

It was the middle of September, and there was a feeling of autumn in the air. The nights were getting longer, and round the fire, as the stars came out, the grown-ups had been talking about the coming winter. Unfortunately, nobody asked the youngsters for their opinion!

The winter had never been a problem to Tom and Emily and their parents. They were used to cold weather in the Scottish Highlands. Even now they had a new baby, little golden Lily, to look after they could stock their roomy cave with stores of food and firewood and snuggle down in shelter through the worst of the weather. But Ollie and Alice had never lived in a cave. Their family had travelled a lot, and had always flown south for the winter. They had never lived so long in one place before. They had enjoyed their summer in the Highlands, living near to another dragon family with very little risk of discovery by Humans, but their woodland camp would be little use in the snow.

Tom was depressed at the thought of losing Ollie, and he knew — though they never talked about it — that Emily felt the same about Alice. He could remember living in their old cave, and Emily talking on and on about how she would love to have a friend. It was because of this longing that they had managed to find Ollie and his family and bring them up to live by the second loch. Deep down, Tom knew that he had Emily to thank for his friend Ollie, but, being a little brother, he would never dream of telling her so!

He was just about to propose a swim in the loch to try to cheer Ollie up, when he caught a whiff of smoke drifting up past the branches of their hiding place. He nudged Ollie and they both peered down. At the foot of the tree Emily and Alice were huffing smoke up the trunk towards them.

Ollie scowled. "Peace or war?" he said.

Alice rolled her eyes in exasperation. "Peace! We want to talk to you."

"You can come up if you like," Tom offered.

"No thanks," said Emily. "You come to ours. There's more room. We have bumbugs and ginger fizz," she added, knowing Tom's weakness.

The boys exchanged glances. "OK," said Ollie, "but no kids allowed." He hated having to look after Lily or his own little brother Georgie.

"Just us," Alice agreed, "a council of war!"

The two boys climbed awkwardly through the branches and launched themselves to the ground, trying to ignore the superior smirks of the girls as they landed in a tangle of tails and wings.

They decided to creep through the bushes round the back of the camp instead of flying, as there was less change of being spotted by Georgie. Then one by one, they flew up to the landing branch and scrambled inside. Emily, the last, pulled the bracken door shut behind them.

"Do sit down," said Alice politely, pointing to the neat piles of new dry heather on the floor.

"This is our place as well," Ollie pointed out grumpily, but he and Tom sat down as Emily brought mugs of ginger fizz and placed a pile of stripy bumblebugs on a large dock leaf on the floor between them.

"Right," said Alice. "I suppose we all know that Mum and Dad are thinking of leaving for the winter. They don't think we can survive up here in the woods."

"We manage," said Tom. "It's not that bad. It's great when it snows!"

"We've got a cave," said Emily. "I wouldn't like to spend the winter in the open. But couldn't you come and share our cave in the worst of the weather?"

"It's too small," said Ollie, sounding unusually grown up and sensible. "Remember that night we all stayed during the thunderstorm? You could hardly move! I think Grandad is the main problem. He wasn't very well last winter, and we lived down south where there was hardly any snow. Then there's Georgie. I can see why Mum and Dad think we should leave, though I don't particularly want to. This is the best place we've ever lived in!" Alice nodded agreement.

Tom felt very downcast. "It'll be awfully boring with just Emily."

Emily refused to quarrel — things were far too serious. She was very fond of Old George, Alice's grandfather, and couldn't bear the thought that he might get ill over the winter. She suddenly had an idea. "There's our old cave!" she exclaimed. "It's not that far away. It's a bit small, but if you're only there for a few weeks it might do. Perhaps they'd let you two stay with us — that'd leave more room. Let's see what they say!"

She was so excited by her idea that she got up ready to fly down and suggest it right away, but for once it was Tom who thought of a snag.

"What about the Humans?" he said.

"Were there Humans there?" Alice sounded shocked.

"No, but they were starting to build further down the glen," Emily explained. "That's why we came here. But we don't *know* that they've found our old cave. It was quite a long way up the glen. Dad said the place would soon be overrun with Humans, but he was probably exaggerating."

"There's only one way to find out," said Ollie. "We'll have to go and see!"

"We'd never be allowed."

"Of course we wouldn't! But if we say we're just going for a flight and a picnic in the hills, they won't know. Then we'll fly as fast as we can to your old cave. We're all strong flyers since we came back from that trip to the sea with Des, and we've had a decent rest since then. We'll be late back and get into a row, but by then we'll have found out what we need to know. Then we just need to talk the parents round." Ollie sounded so confident that even Alice, who was usually the most responsible of the four, was persuaded.

"Are you sure you know the way?" she asked Emily.

"I think so," said Emily, sounding just a little worried. "It would be easier from our cave than from here — a bit nearer too. We'll ask if you can spend the night with us and then we can get a really early start."

"The day after tomorrow," Ollie decided. "That'll give us time to get things ready. How about a swim before you have to go home?"

Feeling a good deal more cheerful, they shared out the last of the bumblebugs, squeezed one by one through the doorway and took off from the landing branch.

At the side of the loch they found little Georgie playing in the shallows watched over by Old George. He was whirling round in circles, sweeping the water with his tail and flapping his wings.

George waved as they came in to land.

"I saw you come out of the tree house together," he said, pleased. "That must mean the latest quarrel is over?"

"Suppose so," said Tom, following Ollie into the deeper water. They both dived and disappeared.

"Allie, Allie!" shouted Georgie, and Alice waded in to rescue her little brother as he tripped and fell, spluttering, into the water. Emily sat down beside George and heaved a heavy sigh.

"You'll miss Alice when we have to leave," he said sympathetically. Emily looked up into his wise kindly face and wished she could tell him about their plan. Even though it had been partly her idea, she couldn't help worrying. What if she couldn't find the way after all? What if they found that Humans had discovered the cave already? No, she couldn't ask his advice. He would be bound to tell their parents and then they'd never be allowed to go.

She forced herself to smile at him. "Of course I will," she said. "I'll miss all of you, even Ollie. But you'll come back when the winter's over. And you never know — you may not have to go at all!"

She got up and splashed her way into the loch to help Alice, who was giving Georgie a ride into the deeper water.

George watched her go, and heaved a sigh of his own. "Oh, I think we will...." he said sadly to himself.

For more information on the Dragon Tales books, email info@alisonjones.com.

Made in the USA
Charleston, SC
08 April 2015